DOCTOR PROCTOR'S F.A.R.T. POWDER

DOCTOR PROCTOR'S F.A.R.T. POWDER

TIME-TRAVEL BATH BOMB

JO NESBØ

SIMON AND SCHUSTER

First published in Great Britain in 2011 by
Simon and Schuster UK Ltd, a CBS company
First published in the USA in 2011 as
Doctor Proctor's Fart Powder: Bubbles in the Bath by Aladdin,
an imprint of Simon & Schuster Children's Publishing Division
Originally published in Norway in 2008 as
Doktor Proktor's Tidsbadekar by H. Aschehoug & Co.

This edition published in Great Britain in 2012 by Simon and Schuster UK Ltd,
A CBS COMPANY

1 3 5 7 9 10 8 6 4 2

Simon & Schuster UK Ltd
1st Floor, 222 Gray's Inn Road
London
WC1X 8HB

Simon & Schuster Australia, Sydney
Simon & Schuster India, New Delhi

A CIP catalogue record for this book is available from the British Library.

PB ISBN: 978-0-85707-633-5
eBook ISBN: 978-0-85707-713-4

Printed and bound by CPI Group (UK) Ltd, Croydon, CR0 4YY

www.simonandschuster.co.uk
www.simonandschuster.com.au

DOCTOR PROCTOR'S F.A.R.T. POWDER

The Postcard from Paris

THERE WAS TOTAL silence in the gymnasium. Nothing was making a sound – not the twelve sets of brown wooden climbing bars along the walls, not the old pommel horse covered in cracked leather or the eight grey well-worn ropes hanging motionless from the ceiling or the sixteen boys and girls who made up the Dølgen School Marching Band and who were now all staring at Conductor Madsen.

"Ready . . ." Mr Madsen called out. He raised his baton and squinted at them through his dark sunglasses. Mr Madsen, with dread in his eyes, searched hopefully for Nilly. He knew the other kids in the band teased the red-headed trumpet player because he was so tiny, which of course he was. But, unlike the other band members, the little guy had some musical ability. Maybe he could turn things around today. Since Mr Madsen didn't see Nilly, he looked over at the only friend Nilly had – Lisa, who played the clarinet. She was the only one in the band who always practised at home. Maybe there was hope after all.

"Set . . ."

Everyone put their instruments to their lips. It was so quiet that the sounds of the warm October afternoon outside could be heard: birds singing, a lawn mower humming and the laughter of little, snotty-nosed kids playing. But inside the gym it was dark. And it was going to get even darker.

"Go!" Mr Madsen yelled, swinging his baton in a majestic arc.

At first nothing happened, and still the only things you could hear were birds singing, lawn-mowing and snotty-nosed kids laughing. Then a trumpet gave a wobbly bleat, a clarinet squeaked timidly and there was a tentative thump on a bass drum. An unexpected beat on a snare drum made a French horn splutter out a belching sound, and in the back of the band something big emitted a snort that made Lisa think of a blue whale that had just surfaced after a week underwater. But all that blowing still hadn't produced an actual note, and Mr Madsen's face was already starting to turn that colour red that warned he was about to lose his temper.

"Two-three!" Mr Madsen screamed, swinging his

baton as if it were a whip and the band members were the slave crew manning the oars of a Roman galley. "Well, play for Heaven's sake! This is supposed to be the Marseillaise, the French national anthem! Give it some dignity!"

But there was no dignity in this. The faces in front of Mr Madsen stared stiffly at the music on the stands in front of them or their eyes were squeezed shut, as if they were sitting on the toilet, straining.

Mr Madsen gave up and dropped his arms just as the tuba finally emitted a sound – a deep, forlorn mooing sound.

"Stop, stop!" Mr Madsen yelled, and then waited until the tuba ran out of air again. "If anyone from France had just heard you guys, they would have beheaded you first and then burned you at the stake. Let's show some respect for the Marseillaise!"

As Mr Madsen continued to chew them out, Lisa leaned over to the seat next to her and whispered, "I

brought that postcard from Doctor Proctor. There's something weird about it."

The voice that answered her came from behind a beaten-up trumpet. "If it's like the last one, sounds like a normal postcard if you ask me. 'Dear Lisa and Nilly, Greetings from Paris. Sincerely, Doctor Proctor.' Isn't that pretty much what you said he wrote?"

"Well, yeah, but . . ."

"The only thing that's *not* normal about it is that a person who is as weird and eccentric as Doctor Proctor would write such a normal postcard."

They were interrupted by Mr Madsen's thunderous voice. "Nilly? Is that you? Are you down there?"

A voice replied from behind the battered trumpet, "Aye aye, Sergeant!"

"Get up so we can see you, Nilly!"

"Yes, sir, oh great commander of delightful music and all the notes of the universe!"

And a little red-headed boy with big freckles and a

broad grin jumped up from behind the music stand, onto the chair. Actually, he wasn't just small, he was tiny. And his hair wasn't just red, it was bright red. And his grin wasn't just broad, it practically split his little head in two. And his freckles weren't just big, they were . . . well, all right, they were just big.

"Play the Marseillaise for us, Nilly!" Mr Madsen growled. "The way it's supposed to be played."

"By your command, great mother of all conductors and king of all military band leaders north of the Sahara and east of the—"

"Stop wasting our time and start playing!"

So Nilly started playing. A warm, resounding melody welled up under the roof of the gymnasium and out of the window on this warm autumn afternoon. When they heard the beautiful music, the birds fell silent, feeling ashamed of their own songs. At least that's what Lisa was thinking as she sat there listening to her tiny neighbour and very best friend playing his grandfather's old trumpet. Lisa liked her clarinet, but somehow there was something special about the trumpet. And it wasn't that hard to play, either. Nilly had taught her to play one song on the trumpet, the Norwegian national anthem. Of course, she didn't play it as well as Nilly, but secretly she dreamed that one day she would play *their* national anthem in front of a big audience. Imagine it! But imagining is imagining and dreaming is just dreaming.

"Good, Nilly!" called Mr Madsen. "And now let's all join in with Nilly! One, two, three!"

And the Dølgen School Marching Band joined in. Staggered, tripped and stumbled in. Drums, saxophones, French horn, glockenspiel and cymbals. It sounded like someone had turned a kitchen upside down and now everything was tumbling out of the cupboards and drawers. Then the bass drum and tuba got going. The whole room started shaking. The wooden climbing bars on the wall started chattering, the ropes were hanging at an angle as if there were near gale-force winds, and the worn pommel horse starting hopping across the floor, inching its way towards the exit as if it were trying to escape.

When they finally finished the Marseillaise, everything became quiet, both inside the gym and out. No birds were singing, no children laughing. There was just the echo of the evil twins' – Truls and Trym – final desperate blows to the drumheads and the eardrums.

"Thanks," Mr Madsen moaned. "I think that's enough for today. I'll see you guys on Monday."

"I'M SERIOUS. THERE'S something stranger about this new card!" Lisa said as she and Nilly were walking home along Cannon Avenue. It was starting to get dark earlier as winter approached, and they liked that, especially Nilly. He thought the light summer nights they had this far north were a drag, kind of a below-average invention. But the warm, dark autumn nights with lots of darkness to provide cover for a little bit of neighbourhood apple stealing – that was a brilliant invention. Actually, it was almost as good as something Doctor Proctor might come up with. Because, in Nilly's opinion, the professor was the best inventor in the world. True, the rest of the world didn't think Doctor Proctor had invented anything of any value, but what did they know? Who invented the strongest fart powder in the world, for example?

Of course, what was even more important was that Doctor Proctor made the best jelly in the world, he was the world's best friend and neighbour and he had taught Nilly and Lisa that they shouldn't let it bother them that the rest of the world thought they were a team of pathetic losers. A team consisting of a tiny boy with red sideburns, a timid girl with pigtails and a much-crazier-than-average professor with sooty motorcycle goggles.

"We know something they don't," Doctor Proctor

liked to say. "We know that when friends promise never to stop helping each other, one plus one plus one is much more than three."

Truer words had never been spoken. But it had to be said that as a friend, the professor wasn't much of a letter writer. They had received only a couple of measly postcards in the three months that had passed since the professor had climbed on his motorcycle, put on his leather helmet and said goodbye as he left Oslo to drive to Paris, determined to find the great love of his life, Juliette Margarine.

Doctor Proctor had lost her under mysterious circumstances many, many years before when he had been a student in France. Lisa and Nilly had only seen a picture of Juliette, from back when she and Doctor Proctor had been dating, on the wall of the professor's lab. But they had looked so happy in the picture that it brought tears to Lisa's eyes. Lisa had actually been the one to convince the doctor to go back and look for her.

"This one is *too* strange!" Lisa insisted. "Just look for yourself."

Nilly looked at the postcard she handed him.

"Hm," he mumbled. He stopped right under the next streetlight and studied it intently while mumbling several *hms* which all sounded thoughtful and intelligent.

"It's from Paris," Lisa said, pointing to the black-and-white picture that looked like it had been taken on an overcast morning. It showed a large, open square and, aside from a bunch of people walking around with parasols and top hats, the square seemed strangely empty. The only way you could tell that it was actually the world-renowned capital of France was that the word PARIS was printed across the bottom of the picture.

"Are you seeing what I'm seeing?" Nilly mumbled, lost in thought.

"Which is what?"

"That it seems like something is missing from this square. Well, I guess, I mean in the picture as a whole."

"Maybe," Lisa said. And when she thought about it, she realised that Nilly was right, but she couldn't quite put her finger on what it was.

"Plus, the card is a little warped . . ." Nilly said, carefully pinching it. "Like it somehow got soaking wet and then dried out again. So, tell me, were you standing in the shower when you read this?"

"Obviously not," Lisa said. "It was like that when it got here."

"Aha!" Nilly exclaimed, raising a tiny index finger that had a bitten-down nail. "I, Mastermind Nilly, have yet again cleverly come up with what must surely be the answer to this riddle. This card must've got wet in his lab in Paris!"

Lisa rolled her eyes. "And how do you know that?"

"Elementary, my dear Lisa. It says so right here on the card. Read it for yourself." Nilly passed the card back to her.

But Lisa didn't need to read it. She had already

read the short message twelve times and knew it by heart. But since you haven't read the postcard, here it is:

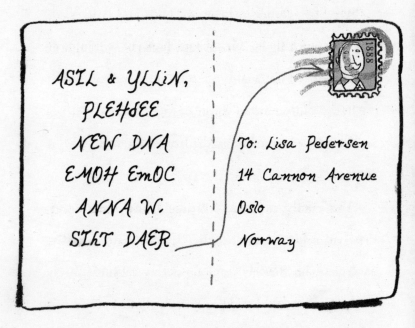

ASIL & YLLIN,
PLEHJEE
NEW DNA
EMOH EmOC
ANNA W.
SIhT DAER

To: Lisa Pedersen
14 Cannon Avenue
Oslo
Norway

"He says he's working on some kind of new DNA invention, right? I'm sure there's lots of ways a post-card could get wet in a laboratory. So what?" Nilly asked. Feeling satisfied, he passed the card back and studied the rest of his bitten-down nails, looking for something new to sink his teeth into.

"It's not how it got wet that's strange," Lisa said. "It's what he's written! Like, for example, who are Asil and Yllin?"

"Maybe he forgot our names," Nilly said.

"That's not it. He wrote Lisa Pedersen just fine in the address," Lisa said.

"Hm," Nilly mumbled, and it didn't sound quite as intelligent as his earlier *hm*s.

"Asil is Lisa spelled backwards," Lisa realised.

"Elementary, my dear," Nilly said, and then he quickly tried reading it backwards. Asil was indeed Lisa. "Well but then what's Yllin?" he asked.

"Guess!" Lisa groaned, rolling her eyes.

"Hm . . . maybe Lisa upside down?"

"It's 'Nilly' backwards!"

"Heh heh," Nilly said, flashing a row of tiny zigzag teeth. "Just kidding. Elementary!" But his earlobes were a tad red. "Well, then the problem is solved. So what are you going on and on about?"

"That's not what's strange!" Lisa shouted in exasperation.

"So what *is* strange then?"

"The rest of what he's written!"

Nilly flung up his short arms. "He told us he's working on some kind of new DNA project. He's a crazy scientist inventor guy, isn't he? The plehdee is a kind of French platypus. They're very unique animals. They're the only mammals that lay eggs. Plus they're one of the only venomous mammals. I'm sure Doctor Proctor could learn a lot from their DNA. Platypuses are all over the place in Australia, but the French ones are on the verge of extinction. There used to be lots of them swimming around in the Seine, but they're kind of absent-minded and there's so much boat traffic on the river, what with all the tourist cruises, that the poor plehdees keep getting bonked on the head by the boats. Anyway, it's really not that strange that an inventor who happened to be in Paris would see what he could learn from platypus DNA, is it?"

"A French platypus?" Lisa said, sounding sceptical.

"Yup," Nilly said. "Featured on page six hundred and twenty of *Animals You Wish Didn't Exist*."

Lisa sighed. Nilly often referred to this enormous book that his grandfather had apparently had on his bookshelf – *Animals You Wish Didn't Exist*.

"Well, what about EMOH EmOC?" Lisa asked. "What's that supposed to mean?"

"Simple," Nilly said. "EMOH EmOC is the actual section of DNA code that Doctor Proctor discovered. Maybe that's what makes the platypus venomous."

Lisa gave Nilly a dubious look. "And who's this ANNA W. person? Didn't the professor go to France to find Juliette Margarine?"

Nilly shrugged. "Maybe Anna's just a friend or some-one who's helping him with his research or something."

"Rubbish! Baloney!" Lisa growled. "First of all, why would the professor go all the way to Paris to search for his long-lost Juliette and then spend all his time with someone named Anna? Second of all, I don't think PLEHdEE is spelled right. If it's French, wouldn't it be spelled *plûdille* or something? And if the professor were studying it, wouldn't he know how to spell it?"

"Hm," Nilly said, scratching his left sideburn and sounding even less thoughtful and intelligent than he had during his earlier *hm*s.

Lisa sighed, sounding discouraged. "And what's the last part supposed to mean, the part that says *SIhT DAER?*"

Nilly chuckled condescendingly. "Ah, but my dear peanut brain, that's the easiest one of all to figure out. Obviously he means 'sit there'. The doctor obviously trained one of the plehdee . . . plehdees . . . plaudeux? I'm not very good with French plurals, but anyway you get my point. He must have trained one of them to sit on command and, drenched after a nice swim in the Seine, the platypus obviously sat on the postcard and got it all wet. Okay, so maybe it's a little bit gross that a wet platypus has been sitting on this postcard, but obviously it's not like it's *dangerous* or anything."

"Enough already, Nilly!" Lisa warned.

Nilly looked at her as if he had no idea what she meant, but obediently kept quiet.

"There's something else here," she said.

"Really?" Nilly asked. "What else?"

"I don't know, but something. Like that stamp, for example. Don't you think there's something weird about it?"

"Nope, I have to say that a square stamp with a perforated edge and a picture of a serious-looking guy doesn't exactly make me jump out of my chair in surprise."

"But did you see what it says on the stamp?"

"No," Nilly was forced to admit. Lisa passed the card back to him.

"Felix Faure," Nilly read. "Well, that's obviously the name of the guy. And 1888, that's probably the year of the stamp. Ew!"

"Ew?" Lisa asked.

"Yeah, imagine licking a stamp that's over a hundred years old . . ."

"Okay, whatever, but do you think it looks like it's a hundred years old?"

Nilly studied the stamp closely and had to admit that Lisa was definitely on to something. Aside from the fact that it was a little warped from being wet, it looked brand-new. The colours weren't faded and the edges looked crisp and fresh.

"Maybe it's a fake, or a reproduction," he said, but he didn't sound quite so confident anymore.

"You think?" Lisa asked.

Nilly shook his head as if to say *maybe not*. "Yeah, there is something more here," he said.

"Everything about this is upside down," Lisa said.

"I thought you just said everything was *backwards*," Nilly pointed out.

"What did you just say?" Lisa asked.

"What you said."

"Which was?"

"That everything was backwards," Nilly said. "You know, the writing."

"That's it," Lisa said, snatching the card back from him. "That's it!"

She studied it. And then gasped.

"What is it?" Nilly asked, concerned.

"I think . . . I think Doctor Proctor's in danger," she stammered, suddenly very pale. "Read the whole card backwards."

Nilly did. And you can too, of course. Right now, for instance . . .

DONE? DID YOU understand it?

All right, neither did Nilly, really. "*READ ThIS*," he read. "*W ANNA COmE HOME AND WEN EEdHELP, NiLLY & LISA.*"

"So that's what it says," Lisa moaned. "Something is very wrong."

"Yeah," Nilly said. "ANNA W isn't actually a name, it means WANNA. And it should be WE NEED instead of WEN EED."

"Not that!" Lisa cried out. "Don't you get anything?"

"Uh, no," Nilly admitted, scratching his sideburns. "For example, I don't get what he means by READ ThIS. The card? We did that."

Lisa stared at the postcard, concentrating hard. "Look at the arrow," she said. "It's pointing at the stamp."

Nilly stuck his right index finger into his right ear and twisted it round and round while squeezing his right eye shut. This always helped Nilly think – it was like turning the ignition key in a car; it sort of started his brain. There was an audible *pop* sound when he pulled his finger back out.

"I've got it," Nilly said, examining his finger with fascination. "The card is a secret message to us, something no one else is supposed to find out about. Doctor Proctor knew that a smart guy like me would realise that there was something strange about the way it was written."

Lisa rolled her eyes, but Nilly pretended not to notice.

"READ ThIS and an arrow pointing to the stamp," he continued. "That means that the rest of the message is under the stamp! We just have to take it off."

"That is exactly what I have been thinking for a while now," Lisa said.

Nilly passed the card back to Lisa with a satisfied sniff. "Good thing you have me here to crack these secret codes, don't you think?"

Doctor Proctor's Cellar

LISA'S FATHER, THE Commandant, woke up on his sofa with the taste of newspaper ink in his mouth. This was because, as usual, he had fallen asleep with the newspaper over his face and was snoring so vigorously that the curtains over by the window were swaying and the bottom page of the paper – the one with the weather on it – was being sucked into his mouth each time he inhaled. He glanced over at the clock and gave a contented sigh when he saw that it was almost time for bed. But first a chicken sandwich. Or two. He tossed the newspaper onto the coffee table and hefted his large stomach out over the edge of the sofa, thus automatically tipping himself up onto his feet.

"Hi there," he said when he walked into the kitchen. Lisa was standing by the counter and Nilly was standing on a chair next to her. The Commandant knew him as the tiny neighbour boy from the strange family that had moved onto Cannon Avenue that spring. The kettle in front of Lisa and Nilly was quivering and sputtering as steam spewed out of its spout.

"Tell me, aren't you kids a little young to be drinking coffee?" the Commandant asked them with a yawn. "And at this late hour?"

"Aye aye, *el commandante*," Nilly said. "We're not making coffee."

Only then did the Commandant notice that Lisa was holding something that looked like a postcard in the cloud of steam billowing up from the kettle.

"What are you guys up to?"

"Go back to the living room, Dad," Lisa said.

"Hey, I'm the Commandant here!" the Commandant said. "I want to know what you two are up to!"

"Sorry, *el commandante*," Nilly said. "This is so top secret that if we told you, you would know too much. And you know what happens to people who know too much, right?"

"What?" the Commandant asked, putting his hands on his hips.

"They get their tongues cut out so they can't speak. And all the fingers on their right hands cut off so they can't write."

"And what if you guys discover that I'm left-handed?" the Commandant said.

"Then you'll be really unlucky, because then

we'll have to remove the fingers from that hand too."

"And what if I can write with the pen between my toes?"

"Both legs right off, *el commandante*. Sorry, but spy work is serious business."

"Yes, apparently it is," the Commandant sighed.

"But everything has a bright side," Nilly said. "Without legs you could lie on the sofa until Easter without having to wax any skis, wash any socks or tie any shoelaces."

"You may be on to something there," the Commandant said. "But what if I figure out that I can put the pen in my mouth? Or send signals in Morse code by blinking my eyes?"

"I'm sorry you figured that out, *el commandante*. Now we'll be forced to cut off your head right from the start."

The Commandant laughed so hard his enormous belly shook.

"Quit fooling around, you two," Lisa said. "Dad, get out of here! That's an order."

Once the Commandant had left, shaking his head, Lisa pulled the card out of the steam. They sat down at the kitchen table and Lisa peeled the stamp off very gingerly with a pair of tweezers.

"It worked!" Lisa exclaimed. "How did you know that steam would loosen the stamp?"

"Ah, just a little basic forensics," Nilly said, but actually he looked a little surprised himself.

"There's something written under where the stamp was, but the handwriting is too small for me to read it," Lisa said, holding the postcard closer to the light. "Maybe it would be easier for you since you're . . . uh, smaller?"

"What does that have to do with anything?" Nilly asked, looking at her with one eyebrow raised.

Lisa shrugged. "Smaller people wear smaller clothes

sizes and are happy with smaller cars. Why not smaller print, too?"

"Let me see it," Nilly mumbled, grabbing the card and squinting at it intently.

"Nada," he said, and held out his hand without looking at Lisa. "Magnifying glass please."

Lisa darted over to a drawer, found her mother's magnifying glass and placed it in Nilly's outstretched hand.

When he saw what it said, Nilly said, "Aha." Because what he saw was this:

SOS. I've disappeared in time. Bring the jar labelled "time soap bath bomb" from the lab and come to Paris immediately. Also, bring the French nose clips that are in the drawer marked "Unpatented

Inventions". You can get money for the plane ticket by selling this stamp to the Trench Coat Clock Shop on Rosenkrantz Street. But don't say anything to the storeowner about where you got the stamp from or where you're going. You understand, Nilly?

"Yup, understood," Nilly mumbled, moving the magnifying glass down.

In Paris go straight to the Hotel
Frainche-Fraille. Once you're
there . . .

. . . Sincerely, Doctor Proctor

"Hey!" Nilly yelped. "What is this? The rest is missing."

"It must have been washed away by the water," Lisa whispered breathlessly over his shoulder. "Does it say anything else?"

Nilly moved the magnifying glass down further.

P.S. I hid the key to the lab in a
very clever spot: under the doormat.

"What are we waiting for?" Nilly shouted.

"On your mark, get set . . ." Lisa yelled.

"Go!" they both shouted in unison.

Then they jumped out of their chairs. Lisa rummaged around in the bottom drawer in the kitchen until she found her father's torch and then they ran out on to Cannon Avenue, where darkness and silence had fallen over all the gardens and wooden houses. The moon was curious and peeked out at them as they climbed over the fence surrounding the smallest house and the garden with the tallest grass (Doctor Proctor had been away for a while). They sprinted past the pear tree over to the cellar door and lifted up the doormat.

And, sure enough, a key gleamed in the moonlight.

They stuck it into the keyhole in the old, unpainted door and the metal made a slightly spooky squeaking sound as they turned it.

They both stood there looking at the door.

"You first," Lisa whispered.

"No problem," Nilly said with a gulp. He took a deep breath. Then he kicked the door as hard as he could.

The hinges made a chilling creaking sound as the door swung open. A gust of cold, raw cellar air wafted out of the doorway and something fluttered over their heads and disappeared into the night, something that might have been an unusually large moth or just an average-sized bat.

"Yikes," said Lisa.

"And ew," said Nilly. Then he turned on the torch and strolled in.

Lisa looked around outside. Even the usually welcoming pear tree looked like it was clawing at the moon with witch's fingers. She pulled her jacket tighter round herself and hurried in after Nilly.

But he was already gone and all she saw was total darkness.

"Nilly?" Lisa whispered, because she knew that if you talk loudly in the dark, the noise will make you feel even more alone.

"Over here," Nilly whispered. She followed the

sound and saw that the cone of light from the torch was pointing at something on the wall.

"Did you find the time soap bath bomb?" she asked.

"No," Nilly said. "But I found the biggest spider in the northern hemisphere. It has seven legs and it hasn't shaved them lately. And a mouth that's so big you can see its lips. Check out this beast, huh?"

Lisa saw a very ordinary and not particularly large spider on the cellar wall.

"A seven-legged Peruvian sucking spider. They're extremely rare!" Nilly whispered, excited. "They live by catching and sucking out the brains of other insects."

"The brains?" Lisa said, looking at Nilly. "I didn't think insects had brains."

"Well, that's exactly why the seven-legged Peruvian sucking spider is so rare," Nilly whispered. "It hardly ever finds any insects with brains to suck."

"And just how do you know all this?" Lisa asked.

"It's in—"

"Don't say it," Lisa interrupted. "In *Animals You Wish Didn't Exist?*"

"Exactly," Nilly said. "So, if you'll go and find the time soap bath bomb and the nose clips, I'll work on trying to capture this rare spider specimen. Okay?"

"But we have only one torch."

"Well, why don't we turn on the overhead light, then?"

"The overhead li—" Lisa started to say, putting her palm to her forehead as if to say *duh*. "Why didn't we think of that before?"

"Because then it wouldn't have been so delight-fully spooky," Nilly said, pointing the torch at the light switch next to the door. Lisa flipped it on and in an instant Doctor Proctor's laboratory was bathed in white light.

There were kettles, pressure cookers, buckets and shelves full of jars with different types of pow-der mixtures and chemicals. There were iron pipes,

glass pipes, test tubes and other kinds of pipes —
even an old rifle with an ice hockey puck attached to
its muzzle. And next to the rifle, on the wall, hung
the picture that Lisa was so fond of. It was of a young
Doctor Proctor on his motorcycle in France. *She* was
sitting in the sidecar — the beautiful Juliette Margarine
with the long auburn hair. His girlfriend and the love
of his life. They were smiling and looked so happy that
it filled Lisa's heart with warmth. In the *last* postcard
he'd sent, he had written that he was on her trail. In
the only other card he'd sent from Paris, in June, he'd
also written that he was on her trail. Maybe by now
he'd found her?

Lisa continued scanning the room again and
stopped when she spotted an almost empty jar with
something strawberry-red in the bottom. It wasn't
the strawberry-red that caught her attention, but the
label.

Because it looked like this:

TIME SOAP BATH BOMB

Instructions:

POUR INTO A BATH THAT IS

THREE QUARTERS FULL. ½ CUP

PER ADULT PER TRIP. WAIT UNTIL

FULL SUDS EFFECT IS ACHIEVED.

THEN SUBMERGE YOUR ENTIRE BODY

AND CONCENTRATE ON THE TIME AND

PLACE YOU WANT TO GO.

P.S. REMEMBER TO HOLD YOUR BREATH!

P.P.S. WHEN THERE ARE NO MORE

BUBBLES. THE SOAP WON'T WORK

ANYMORE!

Lisa took the jar down from the shelf and walked over to a big, rusty filing cabinet. She pulled out the drawer labelled "Unpatented Inventions", flipped through the files until she got to *F* and — sure enough — there was a manila folder marked "French Nose Clips".

She opened the folder, turned it upside down and two blue and seemingly completely normal clips fell out. But no instructions. They looked like you would use them for swimming. She tucked them into her jacket pocket and announced, "I found them! Let's get out of here."

She turned round and discovered that Nilly was standing on the workbench with his whole arm down inside another jar.

"What do you think you're doing?"

"Taking a little fartonaut powder, what does it look like?"

"Nilly! That stuff is dangerous and totally illegal!"

"So sue me," Nilly said. "Besides, a normal amount of farting is healthy."

"A normal amount? The last time you took a spoonful of that stuff, you farted so hard you blasted off into outer space!"

"Leave the exaggerating to me please," Nilly said,

pouring a fistful of the light-blue fartonaut powder into a little plastic bag that he tied shut and stuffed in his jacket pocket. "I flew maybe fifty metres up into the air, and that's not that high if you compare it to . . . well, like the Eiffel Tower, for example. You're a girl, which is why you don't have any talent for farting. You girls can hardly even manage to make little mouse farts." Nilly farted an average fart to make his point.

"Did you hear that?" he asked. "Your turn."

"Pff," Lisa said. "I fart too, but only when absolutely necessary."

"My dear Miss Fancy Fart," Nilly said, screwing the lid back on the jar tightly and jumping down. "I officially bet you a ton of sticky caramels that you will *never* fart loud enough that it can be detected by human ears. Better leave the power-farting to us boys."

"Just you wait and see," Lisa said.

"Wait and *hear*, you mean," Nilly said, putting one hand behind his ear. "And what do I hear? . . . *Nothing!*"

They turned off the light, locked the door, stuck the key back under the mat, strolled through the garden and stopped under the pear tree to look up at the moon.

"So, I guess we're going to Paris," Lisa said. "Alone."

"Alone together," Nilly corrected. "And Paris isn't that far."

"It's further than Sarpsborg," Lisa said. That's where her old best friend had moved to.

"Just barely," Nilly said.

"I have to ask my parents for permission first," Lisa said.

"Forget that," Nilly said. "They'll never let you. They'll just tell you to file a missing person report for Doctor Proctor with the Paris police. And then we both know exactly what'll happen."

"We do?" Lisa asked, a little unsure. "What will happen?"

"Nothing," Nilly said. "No grown-up will believe the stuff Doctor Proctor comes up with. 'He's disappeared in time using soap?' they'll say. 'Have you ever heard anything so ridiculous?' That's why the professor sent that postcard to us. He knew that no one else would believe him, right?"

"Maybe," Lisa said cautiously. "But . . . but then, are you really sure that we believe him? I mean, he's nice and everything, but he's a little . . . uh, crazy."

"Of course I'm sure we believe him," Nilly said. "And Doctor Proctor isn't a *little* crazy. He's totally off-the-deep-end insane."

"Exactly," Lisa said. "So how can you be so sure?"

"Elementary, my dear Lisa. Doctor Proctor is our friend and friends believe in each other."

Lisa gazed at the moon for a long time and then nodded.

"That," she said, "is the truest thing you've said in ages. So what do we do?"

"Well, tomorrow is Friday, right? So, now you go home and tell your parents that Anna who moved to

Sarpsborg invited you to spend the weekend with her, that you're going to take the train down there after school and that her family is going to come and pick you up at the train station."

"Hm, that might work," Lisa said, biting her lip. "What about you?"

"I'll tell my mum that I'm going on a band trip to Arvika this weekend."

"A band trip? Just out of the blue like that?"

Nilly shrugged. "My mum won't bat an eyelid. She doesn't keep track of stuff like that. In fact, she'll probably just be happy to be rid of me for a few days. So anyway, tomorrow you should pack a few extra things in your backpack for school, not a lot, just a few little things that start with P. Your passport, a pair of pyjamas, packs of peanuts and stuff like that. Then we'll go to school and pretend like everything is normal, right? But then after school we'll go downtown, to that clock shop . . ."

"The Trench Coat Clock Shop," Lisa said.

"Exactly. We'll sell the stamp, take the bus to the airport, buy tickets on the next flight to Paris, check in and, presto, we're there."

Lisa chewed on her lower lip as she considered what Nilly had said. *Presto this and presto that,* she thought. When Nilly talked he had this way of making things that were actually very complex seem so simple.

"So?" Nilly said. "What do you say?"

Lisa looked down at the jar in her hand. The strawberry-coloured powder sparkled, beautiful and mysterious, in the moonlight. Disappeared in time? Time soap? French nose clips? This was all too weird.

"I think it would be best if we showed the postcard to my dad after all," she said hesitantly.

"Best?" Nilly asked. "If that were best, Doctor Proctor would have suggested it in his card!"

"I know that, but be a little realistic, Nilly. Look at us! What are we? Two *kids*."

Nilly sighed heavily. Then he put a hand on Lisa's shoulder and gave her a serious look. Then he took a deep breath and proclaimed in an unctuous voice, "Listen, Lisa. We're a team. And we don't care if everyone else thinks we're a pathetic minor-league team. Because we know something they don't know." Nilly was now so full of emotion that his voice had started to tremble a little. "We know, my dear Lisa . . . we know . . . we . . . uh, what was that again?"

"We know," Lisa took over, "that when friends promise never to stop helping each other, one plus one plus one is much more than three."

"Exactly!" Nilly said. "So, what do you say? Yes or no?"

Lisa looked at Nilly for a long time. Then she said one word: "Poncho."

"Poncho?" Nilly repeated, confused.

"I'm bringing my rain poncho. You said we can pack things that start with *P* and from what I've heard Paris is crawling with wet platypuses these days. I do not want to be soaked with platypus spray every time one climbs out of the Seine and shakes itself off."

Nilly blinked a couple of times. Then he finally understood that she was agreeing to go.

"Yippee!" he cheered and started jumping up and down. "We're going to Paris. Cancan dancers! Croissants! Crêpes! Crème brûlée! The Champs-Élysées!"

Nilly continued to rattle off Parisian things that started with C until Lisa finally told him enough already, it was time for bed.

AFTER LISA SAID good night to her parents and her father shut her bedroom door, she sat in her bed like she usually did and looked over at the yellow house on the other side of Cannon Avenue, at the grey curtains on the first floor. She knew that soon a reading light would turn on in there, be pointed at the curtains and then Nilly would start his evening shadow play, with Lisa as his only audience. This night his tiny fingers made shadows that turned into a line of kicking cancan dancers on the curtain fabric. And while Lisa watched the shadows she thought about the story

Doctor Proctor had told them about Juliette's mysterious disappearance so many years ago. The strange story had gone more or less like this:

JULIETTE AND DOCTOR Proctor met each other in Paris and fell in love. One night, after they had been dating for a few weeks, Juliette came and knocked on his door and just came right out and asked him if he wanted to get married. Doctor Proctor was thrilled, but he was also surprised, since she wanted them to get on his motorcycle right then, that very night, drive all the way to Rome and get married there as soon as possible. Juliette wouldn't give any explanation for why she was in such a hurry, so the professor packed his only suit and started up the motorcycle without another word.

He actually had an inkling of what was going on. Juliette's father was a baron. And even though it had been a long time since the family of Baron Margarine had been rich, the baron did not think that a relatively unsuccessful Norwegian inventor was good enough for his Baronette Juliette. But now Juliette and Proctor were driving through the night, through France, on their way to get married. They had just filled up with petrol in a village by the Italian border when they came to a bridge. That was where it happened. Exactly *what* had happened, Proctor never actually found out. Everything went black and when he woke up again, he was lying on the asphalt and his throat hurt. A tearful Juliette was bending over him, and behind her he saw a black limousine approaching. Juliette said it was her father the baron's car and that she had to go and talk to her father alone. She told Proctor to drive across the bridge to the other side of the border and wait for her there. Proctor, shaken and discombobulated as he was, did as she asked without protesting. But when he turned his motorcycle around at the other end of the bridge, he saw Juliette climbing into the limousine, which then backed up over the bridge the way it had come and, once it was off the bridge, turned around and drove off. And that was the last Doctor Proctor saw of Juliette.

Lisa sighed. The rest of the professor's story about his early romance had been just as sad.

After he had waited for Juliette on the other side

of the border for three days, Proctor tried calling her at home from a payphone at a café. The baron himself had answered the phone and explained that Juliette had come to her senses and realised that it would be quite unsuitable for her to marry Proctor. That she was sorry, but that the whole situation was so awkward that she'd rather not talk to him – and certainly didn't want to see him again. That that would be best.

Broken-hearted and exhausted, Doctor Proctor had driven his motorcycle back to Paris, but when he finally walked into the lobby of his hotel there was a policeman there waiting for him. He handed Proctor a letter and curtly asked him to read it. The letter said that Doctor Proctor had been expelled both from his university and the country of France on suspicion of terrorism and manufacturing weapons of mass destruction. The suspicion stemmed from an experiment in the university's chemistry lab in which Proctor and another Norwegian student had almost blown up the entire university.

Proctor had explained to the policeman that it had just been one of those things that happen when you're trying to invent travelling powder for a time machine, which is what they had been working on. And that it really had just been "an ever so teensy-weensy gigantic explosion". Somehow his explanation didn't help at all and the policeman ordered Proctor up to his room to pack his bags. Proctor was pretty sure Baron Margarine was behind the expulsion, but he didn't really have much choice.

So, late one night many years ago, a young man, weighed down by a broken heart, arrived in Oslo and eventually moved into the crooked, secluded house at the end of Cannon Avenue. Mostly because it was cheap, didn't have a phone and had actually never been visited by anyone. It was perfect for someone who didn't want to talk to anyone other than himself anymore, and otherwise just spend his time inventing stuff.

From her own red house, Lisa looked over at the

professor's blue house and wondered if everything that was happening now might actually be her fault. After all, she'd been the one who had insisted that Doctor Proctor go back to Paris to try to find Juliette Margarine, hadn't she? Yessirree. She had sent him right into trouble, whatever type of trouble it turned out to be.

Nilly's finger shadows across the street finished their dance and took a bow. Then they did their normal good-night signal, two rabbit ears that waved up and down, and then the light went out.

Lisa sighed.

She didn't sleep much that night. She lay there thinking about cellars that were much too dark, Peruvian spiders that were much too hairy, cities that were much too big and all the things that would surely go wrong.

MEANWHILE, ACROSS THE street, Nilly had one of the best nights of sleep he'd ever had, dreaming happily about flying through the air powered by farts, breaking mysterious codes, rescuing brilliant professors and all the things that would most definitely – at least *almost* definitely – go right. But, most of all, he dreamed that he was dancing the cancan on the stage at the Moulin Rouge in Paris, where an enthusiastic audience and all the dancing girls were clapping to the beat and yelling, "Nil-ly! Nil-ly!"

Trench Coat Clock Shop

MRS STROBE'S EYES peered down her unusually long nose, through her unusually thick glasses that sat on the very tip of her nose and focused on the little beings in front of her in the classroom and latched on to the smallest of them all:

"Mister Nilly!" Her voice crashed down like a whip.

"Mrs Strobe!" the response came crashing back from the tiny student. "How can I be of service to you on this unusually beautiful Friday morning, a morning whose beauty is exceeded only, my teacher and supplier of intellectual sustenance, by your own magnificent face?"

As usual, Nilly's answer irritated Mrs Strobe. His answers irritated her because they made her feel guilty. And also a tiny bit flattered.

"First of all, you can stop whistling that ridiculous tune . . ." she began.

"Not so loud, Mrs Strobe!" Nilly whispered, his eyes wide with shock. "That's the Marseillaise. Aren't we studying French history this month? If anyone from their embassy were to hear you call the French national anthem a ridiculous tune, no doubt they would immediately report you to the president, who would declare war on Norway on the spot. French men *love* to go to war, even though they're not particularly good at it. For example, have you ever heard of the Hundred Years' War they fought against England, Mrs Strobe?"

The whole class laughed while Mrs Strobe drummed her nails against her desk and contemplated the strange little boy who had been in her class since the spring.

"If you had been paying attention instead of whistling, you would realise that the Hundred Years' War in France is exactly what I've been talking about, Mr Nilly. For example, what did I just say about Joan of Arc?"

"Joan of Arc," Nilly repeated, scratching the sideburns by his left ear thoughtfully. "Hm, sounds familiar. A woman, right?"

"Yes."

"A famous cancan dancer?"

"Nilly!"

"Okay, okay. Can you narrow it down for me a little?"

Mrs Strobe sighed. "Joan of Arc was a nice, pious village girl. As a young girl she received a mysterious message to find the French crown prince, who was hiding somewhere in France, and help him."

"Sounds very familiar," Nilly said. "She didn't by any chance get the message on a postcard from Paris with a rare stamp on it from 1888, did she?"

"What are you talking about? Joan of Arc's message came from angels talking inside her head!"

"Sorry, Mrs Strobe, just a short circuit in my tiny, and yet very complex, brain."

Nilly glanced over at Lisa, who had her head down on her desk and her hands over her head again.

"It won't happen again, Mrs Strobe," Nilly said. "So, what happened to this Joan of Arc?"

Mrs Strobe leaned over her desk.

"That is precisely what I was about to tell you. Joan of Arc found the crown prince and they fought the English together. That young teenage girl put on armour, learned to use a sword like a master and led the French troops into battle. To this day, she remains the great national heroine of France. Write that down, everyone!"

"Wonderful!" Nilly exclaimed. "The good girl won. I love a story with a happy ending!"

Mrs Strobe lowered her long, protruding nose so that it almost touched her desk and peered at the class over the top of her glasses.

"Well, there are happy endings and there are happy endings. She was taken prisoner and sold to the English, who sentenced her to death for witchcraft. Then they invited all the inhabitants of Rouen to come to the Old Market Square, where they tied her to a stake, tossed wood on a bonfire, lit it . . ."

There was a high-pitched, almost plaintive outcry from somewhere in the classroom, ". . . but then, just in the nick of time, the crown prince rescued her!"

Everyone turned to look at Lisa, who was holding her hands over her mouth in horror. No one – not even Lisa – was used to Lisa having an outburst like that.

"Look closely at the picture in your history book, Lisa," Mrs Strobe said. "You can see the flames reaching all the way up to the top of Joan of Arc's white dress. Does it look like she got rescued?"

"No!" the class shouted in unison.

"And she didn't," Mrs Strobe said. "She burned to death and they tossed her charred body into the river. Joan of Arc was nineteen years old."

Lisa looked at the illustration in her history book. The girl's face reminded her of another face in another picture. The young Juliette Margarine in the sidecar of Doctor Proctor's motorcycle. Lisa's eyes teared up at the thought of the awful thing that had happened.

"Of course the girl died," Nilly said.

Mrs Strobe took off her glasses. "Why do you say that, Nilly?"

"To be a real hero, you have to be really dead."

The class laughed, but Mrs Strobe nodded at this. "Maybe so," she mumbled. "Maybe so."

And, with that, the bell rang and even before Mrs Strobe got to the *h* in "have a good weekend", the first student was out of the door. Because this was the last class on a Friday and now they were all free.

Lisa was putting on her jacket out in the hallway when she overheard some of the other girls talking excitedly about some party or other that it seemed like they'd all been invited to. Except for her. And Nilly, of course. She'd heard them whispering about him too. That he was so little and strange and said and did such crazy things that they didn't really understand.

"Hi!"

Nilly jumped up onto the bench next to her so he could reach his coat, which was hanging from a coat hook on the wall.

The other girls huddled together, whispering and snickering. Then the bravest one turned to face Lisa and Nilly, while the others hid behind her and laughed.

"So, do you two turtledoves have anything exciting planned for the weekend?"

"First of all, my dear girl, you have no idea what turtledoves are," Nilly said, buttoning up his jacket, which he did quickly since there was room for only two buttons on it. "But, if you do have space in your brain, you can of course try to store the information that turtledoves are owl-like doves with turtle shells that live by scratching out the eyes of their own young. Second of all, we were invited to some horrifically boring party here in town that we just *can't* be bothered to attend. Oslo is such a boring little city," Nilly yawned.

"Boring like you," the girl said, lowering her hands, but it didn't seem like she quite knew what else to say. So she said, "Hello!"

"Yeah, HELLO!" the other girls repeated behind her back. But one of them just couldn't stop herself from asking, "So . . . so what *are* you guys going to do then?"

"We . . ." Nilly said, hopping down off the bench to stand next to Lisa, "are going to the Moulin Rouge in Paris to dance the cancan. Have an exciting weekend here in town, kids."

Lisa didn't look at them, but she *knew* that the girls were standing there gaping as she and Nilly turned their backs and walked out into the glittering autumn sunlight.

NILLY AND LISA walked over to the bus stop and caught the number seventeen to Oslo City Hall. There they got off and found their way to Rosenkrantz Street, which is a heavily trafficked and rather narrow street with lots of shops and plenty of people on the pavements. On one of the narrowest stretches of Rosenkrantz Street, above a door painted bright red, there was a little display window crammed full of clocks and, sure enough, a sign hanging out front that read TRENCH COAT CLOCK SHOP.

It turned out that the springs in the closing mechanism on the front door were so tight that they had to push against them with their full weight. And, even then, they only just barely managed to force the door open. The springs squeaked in protest, as if they really had no desire to let Nilly and Lisa in. Once the two had finally made it inside and let go of the door, it slammed shut behind them with an angry bang. In an instant all the noise from the street behind them was gone and all that could be heard were clocks ticking. Tick-tock-tick et cetera. They looked around. Although the sun was shining outside, it was strangely dark inside the deserted shop. It was as if they'd suddenly walked into a different world. There seemed to be hundreds of clocks in here! They were everywhere – on the walls, on shelves and tables.

"Hello?" Nilly called.

No one answered.

"These clocks all look so old," Lisa whispered. "And

so strange. Look at that one over there, the one with the second hand. It's running . . . backwards."

Just then, a groaning, screeching squeak, like from an ungreased wheel, became audible through the ticking.

Nilly and Lisa both stared in the direction the sound was coming from, the other end of the shop, where there was an orange curtain with an elephant on it.

"What's—" Lisa started to whisper, but just then the curtain was yanked aside.

Lisa and Nilly gasped. A figure came careening towards them. It was a tall woman – taller than either of them had ever seen before – and everything about her was thin, elongated and sharp. Apart from her hairdo, which looked like one of those tumbleweeds that rolls around in the desert and takes root wherever the wind blows it. This specific tumbleweed had taken root over a face whose skin was stretched so tight it was impossible to say how old it was. The face was also decorated with plenty of black make-up and bright red lipstick covering its thin lips. The woman was wearing a floor-length, shiny black leather trench coat, which was unbuttoned, thus revealing the cause of both the grating, squeaking noise and her speed. She had a wooden leg and on the end of her wooden leg she wore a roller skate that was obviously in need of a little oil. With her other foot she kicked herself towards them, stopping all of a sudden, glaring down at them and saying in a voice so hoarse and whispery that it sounded like wind whistling through an old shack, "You're in the wrong place, kids. Out you go."

Lisa lunged for the door in fear, both because of the woman's unpleasant appearance and because of her breath, which reeked of rotten meat and stinky socks. Nilly, on the other hand, stood his ground, gazing at the woman in the leather jacket with curiosity.

"Why is that clock running backwards?" he asked, pointing over her shoulder.

The woman replied without turning around, "It's counting down to the end of time. And for you, that's now. Out!"

"What about that one?" Nilly said, pointing to one of the other clocks. "It's not running at all. Are you selling broken clocks?

"Sea spray!" she replied. "That's just a clock that claims that time is standing still. And who knows? — maybe it's right."

"Time can't just stand still," said Lisa, who had regained her composure.

The woman stared at her. "You obviously don't know anything about time, you stupid little girl, so you ought to keep your ugly mouth shut. Everything in history happens simultaneously, all the time, over and over and over again. But most people have such small brains that they can't perceive everything all at the same time, so they believe things happen consecutively one after the other. Tick tock, tick tock, I don't have any more time for clock talk, so quick: walk!" She spun round on her roller skate and raised her other foot to push off.

"You're contradicting yourself," Nilly said. "If time is standing still, then you have all the time in the world."

The woman slowly turned back around. "Hm, maybe this dwarf doesn't have a dwarf brain. But all the same, you have to leave now."

"We have a stamp to sell," Nilly said.

"Not interested. Out."

"It's from 1888," Lisa said. "And it looks almost new."

"New, you say?" The woman raised her eyebrows, which looked like they'd been drawn in over her eyes with a black, and very sharp, pencil. "Let me see."

Lisa held out her hand with the stamp.

The woman fished a magnifying glass out of her pocket and leaned over Lisa's hand.

"Hm," she said. "Felix Faure. Where'd you get this?"

"That's a secret," Lisa said.

The woman raised her other, equally thin eyebrow. "A secret?"

"Of course," Nilly said.

"It looks like it's got wet," the hoarse, whispering voice said. "And there's a whitish coating here along the edge of the stamp. Did you put this stamp in soapy water?"

"No," said Nilly, who didn't notice the warning look Lisa was giving him.

The woman stretched out her index finger and scraped a long, red-lacquered fingernail across the stamp. Then she stuck the fingernail in her mouth, which was just a narrow crack in her taut face. She smacked her lips. And then both her eyebrows shot up.

"Well, shiver my timbers," she whispered.

"Huh?" Nilly said.

"I'll buy it. How much do you want for it?"

"Not much," Nilly said. "Just enough for the plane tickets to . . . Ouch!"

He shot an irritated look at Lisa, who had kicked him in the shin.

"Four thousand kroner," Lisa said.

"You cat-o'-nine-tails!" the woman shouted in outrage. "Four thousand for a stamp with a picture of a dreary, dead French president?"

"Okay, three thou—" Nilly started, but yelped as he was kicked in the shin yet again.

"Four thousand, right now. Otherwise we're leaving," Lisa said.

"Three thousand plus a clock for each of you," the woman said. "For example, this clock that runs slowly. Especially made for people who have too much to do. Or this one that runs fast, for people who are bored."

"Yes!" Nilly cried.

"No!" Lisa said. "Four thousand. And if you don't accept in the next five seconds, the price goes up to five thousand."

The woman gave Lisa a look of rage. She opened her mouth, about to say something, but stopped when she saw the look on Lisa's face. Then she sighed, rolled her eyes and spat out a resigned, "Fine, you keelhauling, barnacle-baiting urchin."

The woman disappeared behind the curtain on her roller skate and returned with a wad of cash, which she handed to Nilly. He licked his right thumb and started counting the notes.

"I hope you can add," the woman mumbled.

"Simple maths," Nilly said. "Thank you for your business, Miss . . . ?"

"My name's Raspa," the woman said, with a thin, cautious smile, as if she were afraid her face would rip if her smile were any bigger.

"And what are your names, my dear children?"

"Nilly and Lisa," Nilly said, and handed the money to Lisa, who stuffed it into a pocket in her school backpack.

"Well then, Nilly and Lisa, I'll throw in these gold watches."

She dangled two gleaming watches in front of them.

"Cool!" Nilly said, grabbing for one of them, but Raspa pulled it back again.

"First I have to set the time for the time zone you're going to," she said. "So where are you headed?"

"Paris!" Nilly gushed. "The capital of France . . . Ouch!"

His eyes bulged from the pain.

"Oh, I'm sorry. Did I hit your leg?" Lisa asked. "Let me see it. Did I leave a bruise?"

She leaned over towards Nilly and snarled softly into his ear so that Raspa couldn't hear, "The postcard warned us not to say anything about where we were going!"

"So sue me," Nilly mumbled crossly.

"Ah, Paris," the woman sneered, showing a row of sharp white teeth. "I was there once. A lovely city."

"Nah, it's not that great," Nilly grunted, rubbing his leg. "Actually, we changed our minds. We're not going there after all."

"Really? Why not?" Raspa laughed hoarsely.

"Too dangerous. I hear the rivers in Paris are full of soggy, wet, venomous platypuses shaking water all over people."

Raspa leaned down closer to Nilly and breathed her rotten-meat-and-stinky-sock-breath on him. "Well, then, good thing these gold watches are watertight."

"W-w-watertight?" said Nilly, who had never ever stuttered before in his whole life.

"Yes," Raspa whispered, so softly that they could hear all the clocks in the shop ticking. "Which means that you can swim underwater with them. And wear them in the shower. Or, for example, in a bath. Right?"

"B-b-bath?" Nilly said, wondering where his sudden stutter had come from.

"I'm sure you catch my drift, don't you?" Raspa asked, winking knowingly.

"N-n-no," Nilly said. Jeez, was this stutter here to stay?

The woman suddenly stood back up and snatched the watches back in irritation. "As a matter of fact, I should give you something more valuable than this. A piece of travel advice." Raspa's hoarse whisper filled the shop: "Remember that death – and only death – can change history."

"Only d-d-death?"

"Exactly. History is carved in stone, and only if you are willing to die can you change what is written. Goodbye then, children." Raspa turned round and, on that squeaking, shrieking roller skate, she coasted through the shop like a haunted ship and disappeared behind the orange curtain.

"G-g-g . . ." Nilly tried.

"Goodbye," Lisa said, and pulled Nilly out of the door behind her.

To Paris

LISA AND NILLY walked straight from the Trench Coat Clock Shop to Town Hall Square, where they caught the express bus to the airport. An hour later, they climbed off in front of Oslo International Airport and walked into the gigantic departures hall, which was swarming with people. They queued at the Air France ticket counter. While they were standing there, Lisa thought she heard a familiar sound through the murmur of voices, scuffle of shoes and announcements coming over the loudspeakers. The squeaking noise of ungreased wheels. She whirled round, but all she saw was a sea of unfamiliar faces and people hurrying on their way. She sniffed the air for the odour of rotten meat and stinky socks, but didn't detect it. It was probably the wheels of one of those wheeled suitcases, Lisa thought. And jumped when she suddenly felt a hard finger poke her in the small of her back. She spun round. It was Nilly.

"Go, go! It's our turn," he said.

They walked over to an unbelievably beautiful woman with unbelievably tanned skin and unbelievably white hair.

"What can I help you with, ma'am?" she asked.

"Two tickets to Paris please," Lisa said.

"For you and who else?"

An irritated response came from below the edge of the ticket counter. "Me, obviously!"

The woman stood up and peered over the counter. "Ah, right. That'll be three and a half thousand kroner."

Lisa put the money on the counter. The woman began to count the notes, but then stopped and raised her eyebrows. "Is this supposed to be a joke?" she asked.

"A joke?" Lisa said.

"Yes. Some of these notes are no longer legal tender. They're from . . ." She looked at them more closely. "From 1905. They should have been taken out of circulation ages ago. Don't you have any other notes from *this* century?"

Lisa shook her head.

"Sorry, I can only give you one ticket to Paris."

"But . . ." Lisa began in desperation. "But . . ."

"That's fine," said the voice from under the edge of the counter. "Give us one ticket."

Lisa glanced down at Nilly who was nodding at her encouragingly.

When she looked up again, the woman already had the ticket ready and was holding it out to her. "*Bon voyage.* Have a good trip to Paris. I assume there are some grown-ups there who will be meeting you."

"So do I." Lisa sighed and nodded, eyeing the ticket and Raspa's old krone notes.

"What do we do now?" Lisa asked anxiously as she and Nilly walked towards the security checkpoint.

"Relax," Nilly said. "I have an idea."

"You do? What's your idea?"

"For you to go alone," Nilly said.

Lisa stared at him, shocked. "A-a-alone?"

There. Now *she* was stuttering too.

AS LISA STEPPED on board the plane, a flight attendant who smelled nice and had very neat lipstick smiled at her and said, "Welcome aboard. *Two* carry-ons?"

"Lots of homework," mumbled Lisa, who was looking a little lost and alone as she stood there.

"Here, let me help you," the woman said, grabbing one of the bags, lifting it up and wedging it into the overhead compartment between two wheeled suitcases and then slamming the compartment door shut.

Lisa found her seat, put on her seat belt and yawned. This day had already been way too exciting and she had hardly slept the night before. She closed her eyes, and when she did, the words of that woman in the Trench Coat Clock Shop started echoing through her head:

"Only death can change history. Only if you are willing to die can you change what is written."

With that, Lisa fell asleep and didn't wake up until she heard the pilot's voice instructing them to buckle their seat belts for landing. It had grown dark and thousands of Paris lights twinkled and gleamed below them. Lisa knew that millions of people lived down there. And she was just one, a little girl from Cannon Avenue. Suddenly Lisa felt terribly alone and had to bite her lower lip to get it to stop trembling.

After they landed at an enormous airport that was named after some dead president named Charles Something-or-Other, the flight attendant helped Lisa get her bags down, gave her a comforting pat on the cheek and chirped that she hoped Lisa would have a lovely weekend in Paris. Lisa walked down a long corridor, stood on a long escalator, waited in a long passport line, and exchanged the rest of her old Norwegian money for new French money. She was completely worn out by the time she found herself outside the terminal building, sliding her bags into the back seat of a taxi and climbing in after them.

"*Ooh allay-vooh??*" the cab driver asked.

Now, although Lisa could not speak a single word of French, she assumed that the first thing a cab driver would ask was where she wanted to go. Unfortunately, she also realised that in her confusion she couldn't remember the name of the hotel, all she remembered was that it had something to do with potatoes.

"Hotel Potato," she tried, holding on to her bags tightly.

"Keska vooh zaavay dee??" the driver said. His tone of voice made it sound like a question, and he was looking at her in the rear-view mirror.

"Uh . . ." Lisa said. "The Roast Potato Inn?"

The driver turned round to face her and again asked, *"Ooh?"* but louder now. And his voice definitely sounded irritated.

Lisa's head, in which everything was usually right where it was supposed to be, was one big chaotic jumbled mess right now. "King Edward's?" she tried and could feel in her throat that she was about to cry.

The driver shook his head.

"Hotel Mashed Potato?"

The driver spat out a couple of angry French words that probably weren't expressions of politeness. Then he leaned over to the rear door next to her, pushed it open and yelled, *"Out!"* pointing firmly to the street.

"Frainche-Fraille!" came from the back of the cab.

The driver stiffened and stared at her. Probably because the voice that had just said "Frainche-Fraille" did not sound anything like the voice the little girl had had a moment ago. And it also hadn't sounded like it came from her, but from one of the pieces of luggage she was clutching on to.

"Aha," said the driver, lighting up. *"L'Hôtel Frainche-Fraille?"*

Lisa nodded, quickly and eagerly. "Yes, Hotel French Fry."

With a grunt, the driver shut the door again, started the cab and began driving.

Lisa sat back in the seat and exhaled in relief.

Then she heard a whispered voice next to her: "Psst! What about letting me out now?"

Lisa opened the lock on the front of the bag and

pulled open the top of the bag. And then a tiny boy with enormous freckles and a red Elvis hairdo jumped out.

"Oh, delicious taste of freedom, CO_2 and dust particles wafting in the air," Nilly said, sitting down contentedly next to Lisa with his hands clasped behind his head. Lisa noticed that her best friend appeared a little wrinkled, but otherwise he seemed like he was in great shape. "Now then, my dear Lisa, were you very worried about me during the flight?"

"Actually, no," Lisa said. "I slept. What did you do?"

"I read *Animals You Wish Didn't Exist* until the battery on my pocket torch ran out. Actually, now that you mention sleep, there was a section in there about the Congolese tse-tse elephant."

"Tse-tse elephant?" Lisa asked, but regretted it the second it came out of her mouth.

"It's as big as a house and suffers from narcolepsy," Nilly explained. "Which means that it'll just suddenly,

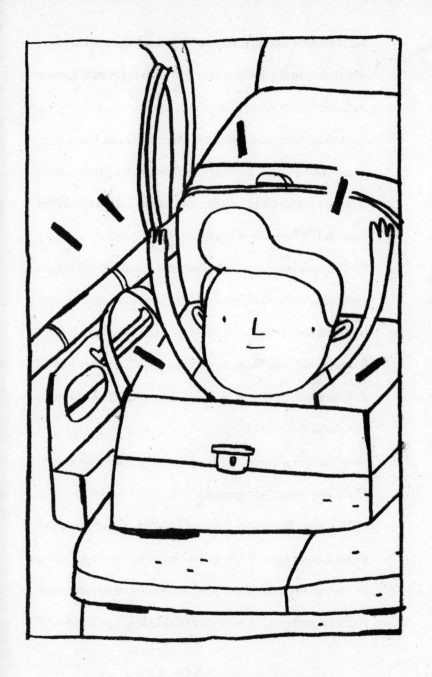

without any advance warning, fall asleep and tip over. So, if you don't keep a safe distance, you risk having an eighteen-tonne Congolese tse-tse elephant flop down on your head at any time. Several years ago, someone tricked a circus into buying a gigantonormous elephant from a little pet shop in Lillesand. What they didn't know was that it was a—"

"Congolese tse-tse elephant." Lisa finished Nilly's sentence, sighed and looked out the window, resigned.

"Exactly," Nilly said. "The elephant fell asleep right in the middle of his first performance and they had to dig three generations of Russian trapeze artists out of the sawdust."

"Oh, enough already. Elephants like that don't exist!"

"They do too! My grandfather told me he saw a couple of them at the zoo in Tokyo. They had just flown the elephants straight there from the jungle in the Congo and because of the time-zone difference, they obviously still had jet lag. One time they fell asleep . . ."

Nilly's mouth kept moving like that until the cab stopped and the driver said, "*Madame* and *Mussyer, l'Hôtel Frainche-Fraille.*"

And sure enough, they had pulled up in front of a tall, thin building that was so crooked you might suspect that the stonemasons had enjoyed a little too much red wine when they were building it. But the hotel had small, charming balconies and a glowing sign that said HÔTEL FRAINCHE-FRAILLE. Well, actually it said HÔT L FRA NC E-F ILLE" since a fair number of the letters seemed to have burned out.

Lisa paid the driver, and they clambered out onto the pavement. In the distance they heard accordion music and the sound of champagne corks popping out of bottles.

"Ah," Nilly said, closing his eyes and taking a deep breath, "Paris!"

Then they stepped through the front door of the hotel. Standing behind the reception desk there was a smiling, red-cheeked woman and a pleasant, plump man, who made Lisa think of her mother and father back home in Cannon Avenue.

"*Bohnswaar,*" the woman said. And even though Lisa didn't know what that meant, she could tell it was something nice, so she responded by saying "Good evening" and curtsying a little. Then she elbowed Nilly, who immediately bowed deeply. She knew a little curtsying and bowing never hurt. This was obviously true in Paris too, because now the two standing behind the counter were smiling even more warmly.

"Doctor Proctor?" Lisa asked hesitantly, preparing for another round of linguistic confusion. But to her delight, the red-cheeked woman lit up: "*Ah, le professeur!*"

"Yes," Lisa and Nilly said in unison, nodding eagerly. "We're here to see him."

"*Vooh zet famee?*" the woman asked, but Lisa and Nilly just stood there staring at her blankly.

"*Paarlay-vooh fraansay?*" the man asked cautiously.

"Why are you shaking your head?" Nilly whispered to Lisa.

"Because I'm pretty sure he's asking if we speak French," Lisa whispered back.

The two behind the counter discussed something between themselves for a while, and Nilly and Lisa realised that French must be a very difficult language even for French people. Because to make themselves understood they had to use their faces, both arms, all their fingers – well, actually, their whole bodies.

Finally, the woman grabbed a key that was hanging on a board behind them, came out in front of the counter and motioned that Nilly and Lisa should follow her as she hurried over to a wooden staircase.

Twenty-six steps and half a hallway later, she unlocked a door and showed them into a room.

It was very plain, with two twin beds, a small sofa, a wardrobe and a desk that was strewn with notes. Plus a door that led into a bathroom that was clearly in the process of being renovated. Or at least on the shelf under the mirror – next to two glasses – there was a hammer, a screwdriver and a tube of glue. There was a bath by one wall and a rusty pipe that was dripping. As Nilly unpacked his toiletries and put them on the shelf under the mirror, Lisa set her backpack down next to the desk in the bedroom. And there, in the middle of the papers on top of the desk, she spotted a drawing. She picked it up. It depicted a bath, just like the one in the bathroom. Under the drawing there were a lot of numbers. They looked like equations, rather complicated equations, actually. They seemed to involve borrowing, carrying, multiplying and dividing, Lisa thought.

"What is that?" asked Nilly, who had just come back in from the bathroom.

"I don't know," Lisa said. "But it sure looks like Doctor Proctor's handwriting."

"And this looks like his motorcycle helmet," said

Nilly, who had opened the door to the wardrobe and picked up a brown leather helmet. "So then these must be his white long underwear."

The red-cheeked and very French woman started speaking French. She gestured dramatically with her arms, repeated the word *"evaporay!"* several times and made her fingers into a bird that flew away.

"He disappeared," Lisa said.

"I got that," Nilly said.

The red-cheeked woman pointed first questioningly at Nilly and Lisa and then at her own mouth with all five fingers.

"And what do you think she's asking us now?" Lisa asked.

"How many fingers we can fit in our mouths," Nilly said.

"You idiot, she's wondering if we want something to eat."

Lisa curtsied deeply and nodded and then firmly

elbowed Nilly, who immediately bowed and nodded as well.

The pleasant woman brought them down to the kitchen and seated them at a table. Then she served them chicken thighs or wings or something, which Nilly thought were really good, whatever they were, before he got so full he couldn't help but burp. All of a sudden he leaped up, bowed politely, something he seemed to have got the hang of, and launched into a long, rhyming apology that made the man and woman laugh out loud, even though they didn't understand a word of it. Then Nilly yawned so loudly that it seemed as if his head would rip in half.

The woman left and came back with two sets of clean sheets that she handed them along with the key to Doctor Proctor's room.

As Nilly and Lisa each made their bed, Nilly commented that those chicken thighs had been so small you might almost think they were frog legs. They both laughed pretty hard at that – because who in the world would ever dream of eating frog legs?

"Hm," Nilly said after a while. "Why does your bed look so much neater than mine?"

"Because it makes more sense to put the duvet in the duvet cover than in the pillowcase," Lisa sighed, walking over to Nilly's bed to help him.

Then they went into the bathroom to brush their teeth.

"How are we going to find the professor?" Lisa asked.

"I'm too tired to think," Nilly said yawning, his eyes half-closed, pushing the screwdriver on the shelf aside so he could grab his tube of toothpaste. "We'll figure it out tomorrow."

"But how can we find him when no one understands what we're saying? And we can't understand what they're saying?"

"We'll learn French tomorrow," Nilly said.

"Tomorrow? Impossible!"

"Even little kids here seem able to learn the language, so how hard could it really be?" Nilly asked and squeezed a white dollop onto his toothbrush, popped it into his mouth and started brushing.

"It takes weeks and months," Lisa said. "And I have a feeling that we don't have much time."

"That's for sure," Nilly gurgled. "We have band practice on Monday."

"Quit joking around, Nilly! This is serious."

She turned to face her friend, who smiled back with gleaming white teeth. Astonishingly white, actually. Yes, whiter than she had ever seen them before – Nilly was not a super-reliable toothbrusher.

"Nilly," she said. "What's wrong with your teeth, Nilly? Well?"

But Nilly just stood there with that grin, which was so stiff that it looked like his bottom teeth were glued to his top teeth. And when Lisa noticed the desperate look in his eyes and the frantic movements he was making with his toothbrush, she realised that that was exactly what had happened. She looked over at the shelf. Sure enough, his toothpaste tube lay there untouched, but the lid on the tube of glue next to it was off.

She picked up the tube and read the label out loud: "Doctor Proctor's Fast-Acting Superglue! You grabbed the wrong tube, Nilly!"

Nilly shrugged his shoulders apologetically and kept smiling that sheepish, idiotic grin.

Lisa sighed and rummaged around in her own toiletries bag until she found her nail file.

"Stand still!" she ordered. "And help me!"

Nilly used both his hands to pull his lips out of the way and Lisa managed to slide the nail file between his teeth on the far left side of his mouth and started filing towards the right. Nilly hummed the Marseillaise as she slowly filed his top teeth and his bottom teeth apart.

"Whoa," he said when she was done and he looked at himself in the mirror. "Check out these pearly whites, would you? And they'll be totally impervious to cavities with this superglue on them, my dear Lisa. No more visits to the dentist for me!" He picked up the tube of glue and offered it to her. "You want to try?"

"No thanks. Why do you suppose Doctor Proctor's Fast-Acting Superglue was sitting right here? Along with these tools?"

"Elementary," Nilly said. "He was obviously renovating the bathroom."

"Maybe," Lisa said with a yawn. "Well, that's enough thinking for one day."

But after they got in bed, Lisa lay there awake, listening to the sound of water dripping in the bathroom, making a sorrowful seeping slurping sound. From outside came the distant rumble of traffic and some wailing accordion music. Plus a sound she couldn't quite identify, but which could have been the creak of a light swinging in the wind. Or, for example, a roller skate on a wooden leg.

Such strange things go through your mind when it's dark out and you're alone in a big city. She glanced over at Nilly. Well, almost alone.

Surely everything would seem cheerier tomorrow.

And indeed, she would be right about that.

The Cancan, Snails
and Margarine

NILLY WOKE UP because Lisa was shaking him.

He squinted at the daylight streaming in through the window and noticed that she was fully dressed.

"It's nine o'clock," she said. "I'm going to try to find a library and borrow a French phrase book."

"A what?"

"A little pocket-sized dictionary with French in it so people can understand a bit of what we're saying."

Nilly sat up in bed. "And how are you going to find a library?"

"I'll ask people for directions. If I just pronounce it the French way I'm sure people will understand: *librairie*."

"No doubt," Nilly said. "What's for breakfast?"

"Nothing," Lisa said. "They only serve air and café au lait for breakfast in this country. I'll buy a baguette on my way back."

"Well, hurry up," Nilly said, swinging his feet out of bed. They dangled just above the linoleum floor and looked as if they were wondering if it was going to be cold.

Once Lisa shut the door, he jumped down onto the floor – which was not just cold, but freezing cold – and sprinted to the bathroom. Shivering, he hopped up onto the chair in front of the sink and looked at himself in the mirror. And staring back at him he found – if he did say so himself – an unusually handsome, red-haired young man of modest physical proportions, but immense intelligence and charm. Indeed, Nilly was so pleased with the boy in the mirror that he immediately decided to give him a warm, relaxing bath on that chilly October morning.

So, Nilly turned on the water in the bath and let it run while he looked for some bubble bath or something similar. When he didn't find any, he remembered that Lisa had brought some soap powder. He found her bag and, sure enough, inside it next to two nose clips he found a jar labelled TIME SOAP BATH BOMB. Nilly grabbed one of the nose clips and the jar of soap, hurried back to the bathroom and poured a little of the strawberry-red powder into the bath.

There's a time for this and a time for that, Nilly thought as he watched the bubbles instantly start forming, growing and rising like a white snowdrift that soon filled the whole bath. Nilly stripped off his clothes, climbed up onto the edge of the bath, put on one of the nose clips and howled, "Bombs away!"

Then he jumped up, pulled his legs in, wrapped his arms round them and plunged into the bubbles. He hit the surface of the water just right and got the maximum effect. Soap bubbles and water sprayed all over the bathroom walls, all the way up to the ceiling. Satisfied, he let himself slowly sink down to the bottom, where he lay, holding his breath and gazing up at the surface of the water. It was covered with such a thick layer of bubbles that only some dim light made it all the way through. And in that light he saw an amazingly beautiful rainbow, like a line of multicoloured, high-kicking cancan dancers at the Moulin Rouge in Paris in 1909. Oh, to have been there!

Just then Nilly felt the bath start to sway beneath him and saw the surface of the water above him start sloshing up and down. As if the whole floor were moving. Yikes, maybe the whole building was collapsing? And wasn't that music he heard?

The floor suddenly stopped swaying. Nilly spun round and stood up in the bath. And remained standing there – completely naked – as the bubbles slid down his body. The music had stopped. And a line of cancan dancers all dressed in red were staring at Nilly. Their faces were at least as astonished as his.

"Where did he come from?" he heard one of the dancers whisper.

"Where did that bath come from?" whispered another.

"What's that thing on his nose?" cried a third.

"Oh, look at how cute he is," giggled a fourth.

Nilly blinked at the bright lights and the audience sitting there with their mouths hanging open too, speechless, as if they had just witnessed a somewhat unexpected moon landing. Nilly didn't understand what was happening. Only one thing was clear: he was onstage at the Moulin Rouge.

LISA STROLLED DOWN a big, broad, tree-lined avenue lined with small clothing stores and perfume shops, but no libraries. She had planned to ask the red-cheeked woman at the hotel before she left, but there hadn't been anyone in reception, just a hippopotamus-like man sitting in an armchair in the lobby reading a newspaper who had eyed her with suspicion and wari-ness. And now she was feeling more and more dejected, because every time she would approach someone to ask for directions they would stick their noses up in the air the second they realised that she couldn't speak French. She was starting to suspect that not all French people were as helpful to foreigners as the man and woman at the Frainche-Fraille. She let her eyes browse the various display windows to see if any of the shops seemed like they might carry books. But it was mostly dresses. Nice dresses, actually. Lisa stopped to look at one particularly remarkable dress. As she stood there, she suddenly noticed something reflected in the shop window, a woman standing across the street wearing a trench coat and big sunglasses. The woman was too far away for Lisa to be able to see her clearly, and yet there was something strangely familiar about her. And even though Lisa wasn't sure who the woman was, it was very clear that the woman was watching her.

Lisa started walking again, pretending to be engrossed in the shopfronts, and sure enough, the woman across the street followed her.

Lisa felt both her heart and her feet starting to speed up. Who was this woman and what did she want? Was it . . . ? Could it be . . . ?

The woman was crossing the street!

Lisa started to run.

There were lots of people on the pavement and Lisa tried darting quickly in and out between them while she kept her head down so that the woman wouldn't be able to see her. And yet, when she turned round she caught a glimpse of the woman's coat between some pedestrians behind her. Lisa ducked into a narrow alley and ran. But she ran only a few metres before she discovered that it was a dead end with a wall at the end. She pressed her back in against the wall behind a drainpipe and waited, staring out towards the main street. There was the coat! It . . . it . . . passed the alley without pausing to look right or left. Lisa exhaled in relief. Now she had to get back to the hotel. The phrase book and baguette would have to wait. But, just as she was about to head back out to the street, she saw the coat again. It had come back and was now stopped right outside the alleyway! It stood there as if sniffing for her scent. Lisa saw an iron staircase leading down to a cellar door below her and scurried down the steps. The steps ended in front of a door and Lisa stood there, waiting and holding her breath.

Seconds passed.

Then she heard a sound from above her in the alley. Someone was approaching.

Lisa pressed down on the door handle. To her relief, it opened! She stepped into the darkness and shut the door behind her and leaned against it with her back. Her heart was pounding like a tap-dancing rabbit. It wasn't so strange that the door had been left unlocked – as far as she could make out, this was a completely empty room. What was strange were the sounds and the smell. It was like an orchestra of squishing, slurping and sucking, as if there were about a hundred invisible fathers eating lamb and cabbage stew in there. And the smell was like . . . like rotten meat and stinky socks. Just then, she screamed. Something wet, slippery and cold had caressed the back of her neck! She ran to the middle of the room and looked around. By now her eyes had adjusted to the darkness enough that she could see that there was something on the walls . . .

something moving, something undulating with long, enormous feelers. And not just over there, but there and there and . . . they were everywhere, they were what was making those sounds, the walls were alive!

As she stood there, frozen with fear, the cellar door slid open. Silhouetted against the daylight outside, she saw the shape of the woman who had been standing on the other side of the street.

"Hi, Lisa," the woman said, shutting the door behind her and flipping a switch. The light came on. Lisa looked around and mostly felt like fainting.

"Why so pale?" the woman asked, coming towards Lisa. "Is it all these giant snails on the walls? They're not dangerous, they just breed them down here. Once they get big enough, they serve them for dinner in the restaurant upstairs. Snails are a delicacy in this country."

"They are?" was all Lisa managed to say, because the woman was so close to her now that Lisa could see her face. And it was definitely a face she recognised.

"Well, Lisa," the woman said. "Maybe you're wondering what these snails live on down here?"

"Uh, what?" Lisa asked, feeling her teeth chattering in her mouth.

The woman laughed. "Grass. And lettuce. Things like that. Why, what did you think?"

Lisa exhaled in relief.

"I'm—" the woman began.

"I know who you are," Lisa said.

"Oh?" the woman asked, clearly surprised.

"Yes, I've seen pictures of you. At Doctor Proctor's house. You guys were on a motorcycle with a sidecar. You're the professor's old girlfriend. You're Juliette Margarine."

The woman in front of her gave her a big smile. "Impressive. And you recognised me again right away?"

Lisa smiled. "No, at first I thought you were Joan of Arc."

"Joan of Arc?" the woman asked, surprised. "The saint?"

Lisa laughed. "There's a picture in our history book at school of Joan of Arc being burned at the stake and I think you look like her."

"Thanks for the vote of confidence, Lisa," the woman said in her slightly broken Norwegian, picking up a lock of her long, auburn hair. "We may have the same colour hair, but unfortunately I'm not a brave heroine, just Juliette Margarine. Which is actually pronounced *Ju-lee-ETT Maar-gaar-EEN* in French."

"Ju-lee-ETT Maar-gaar-EEN," Lisa repeated. "But how did you know my name was Lisa?"

"Victor told me about you and Nilly," Juliette said.

"Victor?"

"Doctor Proctor."

"Doctor Victor Proctor?" Lisa had never thought about the fact that Doctor Proctor must have a first name just like everybody else.

Juliette smiled. "Besides, I was the one who forwarded his postcard to you. Since then I've been keeping my eye on the hotel and waiting for you to show up. You have no idea how happy I was when I finally saw you walk out this morning. 'They're finally here!' I thought."

"But . . . but why didn't you just come into the hotel? Why were you sneaking around after me? And where's Doctor Proctor? And why is everything so secretive?"

"Cliché," Juliette said.

"Huh?"

Juliette sighed. "The answer to most of your questions is Cliché, Claude Cliché, a very bad man, unfortunately. But that's a long story and you look very hungry. Why don't we find a café where we can have a croissant and a café au lait?"

"That sounds great," Lisa said, and then looked around once more and shuddered. Because even if they weren't dangerous, it was pretty unpleasant to be in a room with giant snails covering the walls.

"But," said Juliette, opening the door, sticking her head out and peering cautiously to the right and left, "we should go somewhere where we won't be seen . . ."

Juliette Margarine's Remarkable Story

JULIETTE MARGARINE AND Lisa found a quaint pavement café on a quiet side street and each ordered a croissant. Plus one for Lisa to take back to the hotel for Nilly. But Nilly would have to wait a bit, because first Lisa had to hear Juliette Margarine's story.

"I don't know exactly where Victor is," Juliette said.

"But I was there when he left, and I know what he was thinking. This is a long story, I think I'd better start at the beginning."

"Good," Lisa said, taking a rather large bite of her croissant.

"The whole thing started one Sunday many years ago as I was strolling through Montmartre right here in Paris. There are always lots of painters there offering to paint tourists' pictures for a reasonable price. But in the middle of all these, I came across an eccentric-looking young man I recognised from the university. He was studying chemistry, just like me. I knew that his name was Victor Proctor, that he was a promising inventor and that he came from Norway. I had occasionally had the sense that he wanted to speak to me, but didn't quite dare. But on this day in Montmartre, he came over to me and pointed to a strange contraption – a machine he said he had invented himself that painted portraits in just a fraction of the time the other painters took and for half the price. So I let him – or actually his machine – paint me. But when the painting was done, he looked at it for a few seconds, then ripped it up and groaned in despair. I asked what was wrong and he explained that it was another one of his failed inventions. Because the portrait machine hadn't come anywhere near capturing the beauty of my face. He gave me my money back and was about to leave, but I asked him if I could at least buy him a café au lait for his trouble. We came to this very café that you and I are sitting in now, and we talked about chemistry together until it got dark. Then, we ordered some wine and kept on talking, about our lives, what we liked and what made us happy and about our dreams. And by the time he walked me to the Métro station that evening, I had fallen in love with him and knew that he was the one I wanted. Imagine, I just knew!" Juliette laughed. "All I thought about from that day on was this cute young inventor from a country way up north."

"Cute?" Lisa said dubiously. "Doctor Proctor?"

"Oh, yes, he was quite handsome, you know. I looked for him at the university every day that week, but he wasn't anywhere to be found. On Sunday I went to Montmartre again, and there he was, standing in the exact same spot as the last time, but without his portrait machine. He was shivering and his teeth were chattering, but he lit up when he saw me and we kissed each other on both cheeks the way we do here in France. When I asked what he'd been up to for the last week, he said that he'd been waiting. 'Where?' I asked. 'Right here,' he answered. 'Waiting for what?' I asked. 'For you,' he answered. And from that day on, Victor and I were a couple."

"Ooooh," Lisa sighed. "How romantic!"

"Yeah, it was." Juliette nodded. She smiled a little sadly and drank a sip of her coffee. "But unfortunately, there was someone who had other plans for me."

"Your father, the baron," Lisa said. "He didn't want you to marry a poor inventor. Right?"

"Yes, in a sense that's true, but he wasn't the one who came up with the plan I'm talking about. You see, the Margarine family is an old, aristocratic family. Nobility. My father is a baron. My mother was a baroness and that makes me a baronette. At one time we also had money. All the way up until my great-great-great-great-grandfather, the Count of Monte Crisco, was beheaded by Bloodbath the Executioner during the French Revolution over two hundred years ago. Unfortunately, the family fortune then went to his brother, Baron Leaufat Margarine. He was a drunken lout and a gambling addict who frittered the whole fortune away on Uno."

"Uno?"

"Leaufat lost and lost, but then during a fateful round of Uno in a tavern in Toulouse, when he had been dealt all four of the Wild Draw 4 cards, he became convinced that his luck had finally changed. He bet everything that was left of the family fortune. Unfortunately, it turned out that one of the guys he was playing against, a sneaky swindler named Aigeaulde Cliché, also had four Wild Draw 4 cards . . ."

"But . . ."

"Leaufat lost and in his rage he accused Aigeaulde Cliché of cheating and challenged him to a duel at dawn. But by dawn, Leaufat was so drunk he could hardly stand up. And when Cliché skewered him with his rapier they say more brandy trickled out of his body than blood."

"Ugh."

"You can say that again. There was no money left and our family was only just barely able to hold on to Margarine Castle, which was mortgaged up to its chimneys. Since then we've pretty much just had the title of baron, but not really much in the way of worldly goods."

"But if you're so poor, why wouldn't your dad let you marry a poor inventor?"

Juliette shook her head sadly. "One night my dad came to me and said that he had amazing news, that I had a suitor. And not just any old suitor, but a rich businessman. I was horrified and said that I already had a boyfriend. I mean, he knew that! Yeah, yeah, my dad said, but this suitor had offered to pay off all the debts on Margarine Castle and to restore my family to its former glory. Could my Proctor do all that? he asked. This suitor had come to ask for my hand and my father had already said yes, so the matter was decided. Oh, and by the way, his name was Claude Cliché, my father said, and looked rather alarmed when I screamed at the top of my lungs. You have to understand, my father was not actually a bad person, just a little naive. He must have been the only one in Paris who hadn't heard of Claude Cliché and his gang of hippopotamuses."

"Gang of hippopotamuses?"

"Cliché is a conniving thug who made himself rich by using his gang to threaten people into doing what he wanted. The hippopotamuses are not actual hippopotamuses, they come from a village in Provence called Innebrède. Almost everyone there is related to each other and they all look like hippopotamuses. The hippopotamuses are not very good at doing maths in their heads, but they're very big and strong and they drive around in enormous black limousines. Their job is to copper people."

"Copper people?"

"If you don't agree to one of Claude Cliché's business proposals, like selling your restaurant to him for a ridiculously low price, the hippos come. They say they've come to pay you in copper coins. They fill your pockets with enough coins to buy so many penny sweets that you could fill a swimming pool. Then, they tie your hands and feet, say thanks for doing business with them and chuck you in the River Seine, where you sink like a plumb-bob. And then you stay there, on the bottom, for two months straight, unless someone finds you first."

"Yikes! Didn't you tell your father that this Cliché guy was a crook?"

"Yeah, of course, but my dad just laughed and said that they were probably just rumours, that Claude was probably just like any other businessman. That he couldn't be that bad, my dad had seen Claude and me dancing together at the Christmas Ball."

"You guys danced together?"

"Just one dance. And I only did it because he was sitting at my table and I didn't want to be rude when he asked. I couldn't stand him. He had bulgy fish eyes, a scrawny moustache and thick, wet lips that splattered spit as he bragged about how he'd started out in the business world. It involved two brothers, inventors, who'd just created braces clips."

"Braces clips? I thought those had always existed."

"No, no. In the past people used to have to button their braces. Braces clips were considered a major step forward for humanity, kind of like. . . well, escalators and electric toothbrushes. But anyway, after the hippos paid the two brothers in coppers, Cliché took over their patent and it made him filthy rich. And that's why he always wears braces."

"But, isn't that a little weird?" Lisa asked. "You couldn't stand him and yet somehow he was so in love with you that he wanted to marry you, after only having seen you just that one time."

"In love!" Juliette exclaimed. "Cliché has no idea what love is. There was only one reason why he wanted to marry me: he wanted to become nobility. If he married a baronette, it would automatically make him a barometer. I told my father that, but he made it clear that if I said no, we would be bankrupt and kicked out of the castle. And that I should go and change because Claude was coming to propose to me that very night."

"Double yikes!" Lisa said. "What did you do?"

"I locked myself in my room and thought. And then I realised what I had to do."

"What?"

"Marry Victor before anyone could stop us. The only way to become a barometer is to be the first person to marry a baronette. If a man marries a baronette who's been married before, it doesn't make him any nobler than a mule and it certainly doesn't give him the right to use a title that starts with baron. If I hurried up and married Victor, it would be too late for Cliché and he would leave us alone. That was my plan. I also thought that since powerful criminals like Cliché have eyes and ears everywhere, it would be smartest for us to drive across the border into Italy, where Victor and I could get married in total secrecy. So, I climbed out of my window, went straight to the Hôtel Frainche-Fraille where Victor was living and proposed."

Lisa laughed. "That's what the doctor told me. How exactly did you propose?"

Juliette shrugged. "I knocked on his door. He opened it and said, 'Hi!' I said, 'Do you want to marry me?' He said, 'Yes,' and I said, 'Get your motorcycle helmet, we're going to Rome to get married now.' I didn't give him any explanations. I really didn't want to have to explain to him that my dad, his future father-in-law, didn't want him as a son-in-law and had promised me to someone else instead."

"And what did the professor say?"

"Victor just laughed and did what I said. We climbed onto the motorcycle and he floored it. Out of Paris to the south, towards the mountains of Provence and the Italian border. We drove all night and it was cold, but Victor's scarf, which he'd knitted on a knitting machine he had invented, was twenty metres long, so we wrapped it around both of us."

"How . . . sweet."

"Sweet, yes. But I knew that by now Cliché would have sent out the alarm and dispatched his hippos. I hadn't told Victor anything. Why should I? He was in high spirits, we were already far from Paris and soon it

would all be behind us. As the sun began to come up, we zoomed past a sign with a name on it and into a village. Victor spotted a petrol station and slowed down. I yelled from the sidecar that he should keep going, that he shouldn't stop here, that we could fill up the tank in Italy, that it was only a mile or two to the border. But the engine and the long, flapping scarf were making so much noise that he didn't hear me. So he stopped in front of a big guy in overalls with a cigarette in the corner of his mouth who was leaning against the only pump. Behind him sat another guy who looked exactly like him, tilting a chair back and reading a magazine. Victor said, 'Fill 'er up' and didn't notice that I had unwound myself from the scarf and was hunching down in the sidecar."

"Why were you doing that?"

"Because I'd been able to read the name on the sign as we drove in. And look at those two guys. They had teeth as big as tombstones in those enormous jaws of theirs. They looked like—"

"Don't tell me," Lisa gasped. "Hippos! You were in Innebrède. How awful!"

"The guy in the overalls starting pumping the petrol, eyeing Victor with suspicion the whole time. Then he called over his shoulder to his twin brother, 'Hey, what did the boss say that professor guy looked like?' 'Tall, thin, ugly beanpole with motorcycle goggles,' the brother answered without looking up from his magazine. 'Guy's name is Proctor.'

"I was scared because that meant that not only did Cliché know I'd run off, but he knew who I was with. Meanwhile, Victor, who had no idea what was going on, lit up: 'Wow! Have you guys heard of me? I mean, I knew there was that piece in the school paper about my time-travel bath bomb, and they did take my picture to go with it, but to be recognised so far from Paris, well—'

"At this point I interrupted Victor and whispered as loudly as I dared, 'Drive away! Drive away now!'

"'But honey, Juliette, these nice men just wanted to—'

"'Drive! Otherwise we'll miss our appointment with the priest!'

"'Well, I have to pay for the petrol—'

"Victor hadn't noticed that the hippos were closing in, so I stood up in the sidecar, stomped on the starter pedal and turned the throttle as far as it would go. The motorcycle jumped, lurching forward. And I did a backflip out of the sidecar. I landed on my head on the asphalt as the pump hose arched and danced, spraying petrol all over both of the hippos and me."

"Oh no, oh no!" Lisa exclaimed, leaning so far forward that she was about to tip over her coffee cup.

"Oh yes, oh yes," said Juliette, rescuing the coffee cup at the last second. "I saw stars, but picked myself up and started running – well, staggering – after the motorcycle. With both hippos on my heels. I was spitting out petrol and yelling for Victor, but he couldn't see or hear me, I could see that he was laughing and saying something to the sidecar. He thought I was still sitting in there and was probably getting a kick out of driving away without paying for the petrol."

"Oh no!"

"I thought I was done for. The two hippos were closing in. The one in the overalls with the cigarette grabbed me by the hair. But then I heard a *poof* and he was gone."

"What happened?"

"Cigarette smoking and petrol, a bad combination. But the other one was closing in. I could hear the coins jingling in his pockets. His heavy, wheezing hippo breathing. And Victor didn't seem to be slowing down. He was slowly getting further and further away."

"Double oh no!"

"I was about to give up and then I noticed Victor's scarf. It was dragging along behind the motorcycle. I felt hippo fingers clutching at my back. With the last of my strength, I dived forward, grabbed the corner of Victor's scarf and held on for my very life as I was pulled away."

"But then you were being dragged over the asphalt?"

"Yup. The asphalt instantly wore holes in the knees of my trousers, and it stung like you wouldn't believe. So, I scrambled up onto my feet and kept the soles of my shoes against the ground so that I was being pulled along behind the motorcycle, kind of like if I was on water skis."

"That's the worst thing I've ever heard!"

"No, that would be this next part," said Juliette. "Victor still hadn't noticed what was going on. I was about to lose my grip on the scarf as we came round a bend, heading straight for a bridge. Next to the bridge there was a sign that said 'Gustav Eiffel's Bridge'. I realised that this was my last chance to catch Victor. Without letting go, I scooted to the edge of the road and over to the sign. The next instant, the scarf and I starting whipping round the signpost. That's the fastest carousel ride I've ever been on in my whole life. I was so dizzy that I was reeling when I stood up and saw Victor lying in the middle of the bridge. His motorcycle was stopped a little further ahead. I ran over to my beloved Victor. His face was totally blue, poor thing, his eyes were bulging out and he tried to speak, but he couldn't get a single word out . . ."

"Was he injured?"

"No, it was just the scarf squeezing his neck. Once I loosened it and he was able to breathe again, he talked. True, in a very strange voice, kind of like this . . ."

Juliette mimicked him, speaking in a high, squeaky voice: "Juliette, what happened?"

Lisa giggled a little. And so did Juliette.

"I said it was nothing, that now we would go to Rome and get married. Then I took his hand and we ran to the motorcycle. He got it started, but a valve had been damaged and he said we wouldn't be able to go very fast, that he hoped the priest would wait for a bit.

That's when I saw the wide black limousine coming over the crest of the hill towards the bridge."

"A black limousine?" Lisa said. "Hippos!"

"The limousine was so wide that for a second I hoped the bridge would be too narrow for it. But it just barely managed to manoeuvre its way on to the bridge and was coming straight towards us."

"Surely this was the end!"

"Yes, Lisa. This time it was the end. With a broken valve there was no way we would beat them to Italy. Way down under the bridge there was a river, flowing deep and black. And I knew what the hippos would do if they caught us together."

"Yeah," Lisa said breathlessly. "Fill your pockets with coins and toss you off the bridge."

"Victor, yes," Juliette said. "But not me. They would take me to Paris, put me in a wedding dress and then drive me to a church where Cliché would be waiting, in a tuxedo and braces and that scrawny moustache, waiting for my 'I do' so that he could finally call himself a . . . BAROMETER!"

Juliette slapped the table with her hand so her café au lait sloshed over the side of her cup and then continued in a voice on the verge of tears.

"But, I also knew that if the hippos caught me, they wouldn't worry about chasing Victor anymore. He wouldn't be that important to them once they had me. So I . . . I did what I had to do." Juliette stuck her hand in her purse and pulled up a handkerchief that was every bit as white and daintily embroidered as one would expect a baronette's handkerchief to be. She dabbed away a big, glossy tear. "I lied to Victor. I said that it was my father's limousine, that he must have followed us and that I had to go and talk to him. And that Victor should hurry, drive over the border into Italy and wait for me there. He protested, but I insisted. I pushed him onto the motorcycle, said *au revoir* – goodbye – and he drove away."

Juliette Continues
Her Story

JULIETTE WAS STARING straight ahead. Then she put the handkerchief over her nose and blew loudly, like a trumpet blast and not quite the way one would expect a baronette to blow her nose.

"Three days later I married Claude Cliché in Notre Dame, a cathedral in Paris. People were up playing Uno until all hours that night and Claude lost some money to one of my father's wedding guests. That guest was found a week later at the bottom of the Seine with his pockets full of small change. I think that finally opened my father's eyes to what kind of person Claude is. My father pulled me aside, asked if I was happy, said it would be all right with him if I got a divorce, that we didn't need the castle, that we could live in a small apartment and that he could get a job. Poor Dad! He just didn't understand that Claude would never allow himself to be humiliated like that, that if we so much as mentioned the word 'divorce' we'd both end up in the Seine, Dad and me. So I said, no, I was fine. Of course the truth was that I could hardly stand living with that monster even for a single day."

"Triple yikes!"

"You can say that again. And so the years passed. Dad got old before his time and then two years ago he got sick and died of pneumonia. As we were sprinkling dirt over his coffin, Claude whispered to me that now that my father wasn't in the picture anymore, maybe I might be thinking about running off and finding my professor boyfriend again. But that if I tried that, I would find out what it was like to stand on the bottom of the Seine with my pockets full of coins, holding my breath and just waiting to drown. Then he patted my cheek and said the hippos would be watching me."

"That . . . that . . . bully," Lisa whispered, feeling her eyes well up.

"I had totally given up on having a happy life," Juliette continued. "Until early this summer. Then I suddenly received a strange postcard in the mail. It had a Paris postmark and apart from my name the words on it were totally unintelligible. But I recognised the handwriting right away. It was my beloved Victor's. Just think, he hadn't forgotten about me after all these years! My heart rejoiced. So I sat down and tried to make sense of what he'd written. And do you know what I found out?"

Lisa nodded. "I think I do. It was written backwards, wasn't it?"

"Yes!" Juliette exclaimed. "How did you know . . . Oh, right, I forgot that you got a backwards postcard too."

"How did you know——" Lisa started to ask, but Juliette placed a hand on Lisa's arm and said, "I'll get to that in a second, dear. When I read the card backwards, I saw that Victor wanted me to sneak out and meet him at the Hôtel Frainche-Fraille the following night. He was staying in the same room he had rented so many years before. He wrote that Madame Trottoir, owner of the Frainche-Fraille, had told him about the rumours that I had been forced to marry the worst thug in Paris, Claude Cliché. I was so nervous, I was shaking as I stood in front of his door and knocked. But when he opened the door and I fell into his arms, it was as if we had never been apart!" Juliette closed her eyes and whispered, enthralled, "Oooooh . . ."

"Oooh," Lisa whispered, every bit as enthralled.

"Victor wanted us to run away together, but I explained to him that Cliché was more powerful, richer and had more small change than ever before, and that he would pursue us to the ends of the earth and that, eventually, he would find us. That's when Victor came up with his crazy, crazy idea . . ."

"What idea?"

"The idea of using Doctor Proctor's time-travelling bath."

"Doctor Proctor's what-the-huh?"

Juliette was just about to respond when Lisa saw her notice something across the street.

"We have to get out of here, Lisa."

"What is it?"

"Hippo alert." Juliette put on her sunglasses and left a few coins on the table. "Come on. We have to find somewhere to hide."

Lisa looked in the same direction that Juliette just

had, and sure enough, two people with unmistakably hippo-like traits were standing across the street.

"Nilly!" Lisa said, jogging after Juliette who was quickly striding down the pavement. "We've got to go and get Nilly!"

"Follow me," Juliette said, handing Lisa a stiff little piece of paper that looked like a ticket and turning to descend a staircase that looked like it went right down into the ground.

It *was* a ticket and the stairs *did* go right down into the ground.

"This is the Métro," Juliette said as they stood in a subterranean hall and fed their tickets into a yellow machine so the metal bar in front of them would let them through. They ran through the damp, cool tunnels and down stairs that led them further underground. They emerged on to a platform in a catacomb-like cavern just as a train pulled in and doors slid open. They hurried in. As they were waiting for the doors to close, they heard a distant thudding sound, as if something heavy were running towards them. Juliette didn't need to tell Lisa what it was, but she did anyway: "Hippo feet."

Lisa stared at the stairs. First she saw hippo feet, then hippo bodies and then hippo faces. They stopped running and now they were looking around. One of them shouted something and pointed to the train. To Lisa. She ducked down below the window and stared at the sliding doors, which were still open. "Close, close, close," she pleaded in a whisper.

Then she heard heavy, running hippo footsteps again.

A metallic voice said something over the PA system and then – finally – she heard a snorting groan from the doors as they started to slide shut. Lisa heard angry shouts and someone pounding on the side of the train and then a forceful blow right above her that shattered the glass.

The train started moving slowly. She looked up. Now there was a white pattern on the windowpane.

And an angry face was staring at her from the other side of the window, but not a hippo face. This face had bulging eyes and thick, wet snail lips just below a pencil-thin moustache. A pair of wide braces was stretched across the person's stomach and shoulders. Juliette didn't need to tell Lisa who it was, but she did anyway. In a whispering voice that quaked with fear: "Claude."

Nilly Meets Juliette
and Vice Versa

JULIETTE STARED DUMBFOUNDED at the tiny little boy with the red hair who had just opened the door for her and Lisa. Not just because the boy, who without a doubt had to be the Nilly that Victor had told her about, was even smaller now that she was seeing him close up. He was also naked – aside from a towel around his waist — dripping wet and had a blue nose clip pinched onto his nose. But the most surprising thing was that he had just said *Bonjour, Madame,* which is French and means "Hello, ma'am," as if it was completely natural for him, and his French pronunciation was perfect.

"Je suis Juliette Margarine," Juliette said. *"Et tu es Nilly?"* — which is also French and means, "I'm Juliette Margarine. And you're Nilly?"

"Oui, Madame Juliette," Nilly said in a nasal voice, bowing deeply and opening the door the rest of the way for them.

Juliette and Lisa darted in. Lisa hurriedly locked the door while Juliette took up position by the window, looking down at the street below.

"Cliché's hippos are after us," Lisa said. "We managed to sneak away, but I'm sure they'll be back soon. That guy who was sitting in the lobby reading a newspaper looked suspiciously hippo-like."

"Excuse-moi?" Nilly said.

"I'll explain later. Quick, get dressed. We have to get out of here."

Nilly looked like a wet, human miniature question mark topped with a few bath bubbles.

"Qu'est-ce que tu dis là?" he asked in that strange, nasal voice.

"Speak properly. We don't have time for this nonsense," Lisa said angrily and yanked Nilly's nose clip off.

"So sue me, Miss Shrew, but I don't understand a word you're saying," Nilly said.

"What don't you understand?" Lisa asked.

"Hey, now I understand you!"

"Well it's about time," muttered Lisa, who had already started stuffing her things into her backpack. "Juliette is going to take us to a different hotel. Claude Cliché and his hippos have been spying on her for the last several weeks. They've had the Hôtel Frainche-Fraille under surveillance since Juliette has been here several times."

"That's why I didn't dare come into the hotel and make contact with you here," Juliette said. "I knew one of the hippos was sitting down there in the lobby in case I showed up. So, I stood in the entrance of a building across the street and waited for one of you to come out, so I could make contact. I'm afraid I might have scared Lisa a little."

"Yeah, maybe a little," Lisa said. "Hurry up, Nilly. That hippo in the lobby saw us. They'll be here soon."

"Yeah, yeah. Let me just concentrate," Nilly said as he stared down at the clothes lying on the bed. "Let's see. First the trousers, then the shoes. FIRST the trousers, THEN the shoes. Yes, that's right."

Then he pulled on his trousers. And then his shoes.

"Um, what about the socks?" Lisa asked.

"Darn it," Nilly said, kicking off his shoes again and putting on his socks.

"What have you been doing, anyway?" Lisa asked.

"I took a bath," Nilly said. "And danced the cancan

at the Moulin Rouge. One of the dancing girls thought I was cute."

"Yeah, right," Lisa said.

"It's true," Nilly said. "I just ducked down into the bathwater and when I came up again, I was at the Moulin Rouge. And it seemed like it was a long time ago, because everyone was wearing old-fashioned clothes."

"Nilly, don't you ever get tired of making things up?" Lisa asked, slapping shut the top flap of her backpack. She was ready to go.

"And there I was," Nilly said. "Just as naked as the day I was born, in front of a huge audience and eight super-attractive cancan dancers. Boy, was *that* embarrassing."

Lisa noticed that Juliette was laughing so hard she was shaking as she stood over by the window, keeping her eye on the street below.

"So I jumped back into the bath and submersed myself. I held my breath and wished I was back in the hotel room, here and now. And guess what happened?

When I came up again, I *was* back here, as if nothing had happened!"

"That's because nothing *had* happened," Lisa said. "Aside from inside that weird brain of yours. And meanwhile a lot of stuff has been happening in the real world, so get a move on, would you?"

Before Nilly put the few things he'd unpacked back into his bag, he took out a small jar with a lid with several air holes in it. He carefully placed the jar in the side pocket.

"What's that?" Lisa asked sternly.

"A seven-legged Peruvian sucking spider."

"A what? You didn't bring the . . . ?"

Nilly shrugged his shoulders. "He seemed so lonely down there in Doctor Proctor's cellar. No professor and so far away from all his buddies in Peru, huh? I decided to call him Perry. So sue me. But we did agree that we were allowed to bring small things that start with *P*, right?"

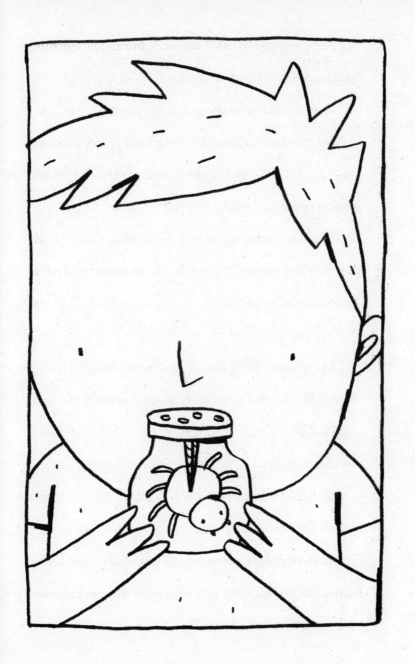

"Yeah, I guess," Lisa groaned. "But hurry up now. And no more making up stories."

"I haven't made up any—"

"Oh, you haven't, have you? How did you understand that that dancing girl said you were cute? You don't happen to speak French, do you?"

They were interrupted by Juliette's calm voice from over by the window. "Hey guys. I have some good news and some bad news."

Nilly and Lisa turned towards her.

"The good news is that Nilly doesn't need to hurry after all. The bad news is that the hippos have surrounded the hotel, so we're not going to be going anywhere."

"Uh-oh," Lisa said softly.

"Uh-oh," Nilly said softly.

"Now what are we going to do?" Lisa said. "The hippos are going to fill our pockets with small change and dump us in the Seine."

"What?!" Nilly protested. "Small change? Those cheapskates. I want big change. I want notes!"

"Shh, kids," Juliette said. "There might be a way for us to get out. But it would mean that you have to listen to me very carefully. All right?"

It seemed like that was fine with them. At any rate, both Nilly and Lisa shut their mouths and looked at Juliette while their ears sort of seemed to curl out from their heads a little bit so they could hear extra well. And a good thing too, because Juliette was about to tell them something that would explain Nilly's strange experience in the bath, how he was suddenly able to both understand and speak French, how Doctor Proctor had disappeared and how Lisa and Nilly might – just might – be able to escape from the hippos and the watery depths of the River Seine.

But you won't be finding out any of that until the next chapter.

Doctor Proctor's
Time-Travelling Bath

JULIETTE FLUNG OPEN the door to the bathroom and pointed dramatically to the bath. It was filled to the rim with water and soap bubbles, even though the bubble layer had diminished quite a bit since Nilly had done his cannonball into it.

"This," said Juliette, her voice quivering, "is a time-travelling bath. You can go anywhere you want in terms of time or space in this bath. All you have to do is fill it with water, get the soap to make bubbles and then submerse yourself. You concentrate on where and when – the date and the time – you want to go. After seven seconds, you can come up again and, voilà, you're there! You can go anywhere you want, but you can't go to the same place more than once. In other words, you get only one chance to change the past at that specific location."

"Cool!" Nilly exclaimed. "When did Doctor Proctor invent this doohickey?"

"While he was living here in Paris, just before he met me. Which is to say, Victor—"

"Victor?"

"Doctor Proctor," Lisa said. "Doctor Victor Proctor, that is."

"*Victor* Proctor?" Nilly spluttered in disbelief.

"Well, he has to have a first name, doesn't he? Just like everyone else," Lisa said.

"Sure," Nilly said. "Doctor, for example. That's a great first name."

"Anyway," Juliette said patiently. "Victor was the one who invented the actual time-travelling bath and his assistant invented the time soap bath bomb."

"Remarkable," Lisa whispered.

"Ha!" Nilly said, folding his arms across his chest. "Now do you believe me? I was lying there on the bottom of the bath thinking about the Moulin Rouge in around 1909, wasn't I? And, voilà—"

"You were there," Lisa said. "Wow, I'm sorry I doubted you, Nilly. You always do tell the truth."

Nilly closed his eyes halfway and gave Lisa a gracious look. "I'm not the kind of person to hold a grudge, my dear Lisa. If you tie my shoelaces for the next week, we'll call it even."

Lisa gave him a warning look.

"Well, well, get into the bath, kids," Juliette said. "Cliché is on his way."

"Are you sure it will work now that there's more than one of us in there?" Lisa asked sceptically, climbing cautiously into the water after Nilly.

"Yes," Juliette said. "Victor and his assistant tested it thoroughly."

"How weird," Lisa said. "If he's had this amazing invention for all these years, why hasn't the rest of the world ever found out about it?"

"Exactly!" Nilly said. "He could have been rich and famous."

"Because the time-travelling bath only works with the time soap bath bomb," Juliette said. "And his assistant was the only person who knew how to make that. They had a falling out, and without the soap Victor didn't have a patentable invention. All Victor had left of the soap was that little jar he brought back to Norway with him when he was expelled from France."

"The jar that was in his basement in Cannon Avenue," Lisa said.

Juliette nodded and held up the jar containing the strawberry-red powder. "He brought a little of the soap from this jar with him when he came back to Paris two months ago, and that's what he used three weeks ago when he stood exactly where you are standing now, said goodbye to me, and travelled back to July 3, 1969, to the village of Innebrède in the Provence mountains to change history."

"To change history?" Nilly and Lisa gasped in unison.

"Nothing less," said Juliette. "The plan was to travel back to Innebrède and be standing there waiting at the petrol station when we pulled in on the motorcycle. He'd hold up a big sign written in Norwegian so that only we could read it, warning us not to stop so we would keep driving all the way to Italy and get petrol there. Even if petrol costs more in Italy."

"Of course!" Lisa said. "Because that would keep all the stuff that happened from happening."

"Exactly," Juliette said. "The hippos would never have noticed us, Victor and I would have got married in Rome, Cliché would have given up trying to become a barometer and Victor and his assistant would have made up again and patented the time-travelling bath and the time soap bath bomb together and become world famous and so rich that Victor could pay off the mortgage on my family's castle."

"But if everything had gone the way it was supposed to with his time travelling, Proctor would have been back by now, wouldn't he?" Lisa asked. "So what could have happened?"

"Elementary," Nilly said. "Doctor Proctor ran out of time soap bath bomb and couldn't get back. That's why

· 155 ·

he sent us that message on that postcard. Although how he managed to send that . . ."

"I was the one who sent it," Juliette said, pouring a little of the soap powder into the tub.

"You?" Nilly said.

"Well, actually, I forwarded it. I sneaked into the hotel room every day to see if Victor was back yet. I sat in the bath and waited, but nothing happened. Until one day suddenly a postcard floated up to the surface. It was addressed to Lisa, whom I'd heard so much about."

"And Nilly," Nilly said.

"And Nilly," Juliette agreed.

"So, that's how the postcard got wet! Some of the writing was washed off and there were traces of soap on the stamp," Lisa said.

"Hm, if you ask me," Nilly said, "that's how the postcard got wet. Some of the writing was washed off and there were traces of soap on the stamp."

Juliette poured a little more soap powder into the

water. "Stir it up and make some bubbles. Quick, the hippos will be here any minute."

Nilly churned his arms like a whisk in the water.

"Why couldn't the doctor just get in touch with that assistant and get more soap?" he asked.

Juliette sighed. "Victor's assistant was a very peculiar person. Right after Victor and I started seeing each other, they had a falling out. I'm not sure why, but after Victor disappeared, his assistant tried to steal the whole time-travelling bath invention. Luckily Victor hadn't left any sketches behind. He kept everything in his head, and Victor himself was the only one who knew how to configure the bath so it would work. And—"

Juliette suddenly stopped talking because they all heard a definite creaking sound from the hallway outside.

"Wha-what's that sound?" Nilly asked.

Juliette held out her hand. It held the two blue nose clips. "Quick, put these on and dive."

"Don't need to," Lisa said, demonstrating how she

could pinch her nose shut with her thumb and index finger.

Juliette opened one of the blue nose clips and released it so that it clipped over Lisa's nostrils with a little *pop!*

"Ouch!" Lisa protested.

Juliette gave Nilly the other nose clip. "Keep them on and a lot will become clear to you."

There was a loud knock on the door.

"Under the water, now!" Juliette whispered, screwing the lid of the soap jar back on and passing it to Lisa.

"But you have to come too," Lisa urged.

"No, I have to stay here."

"What?" Lisa whispered. "Cliché is just going to lock you up again! And we'll never find Doctor Proctor without your help!"

There was another knock on the door, louder this time.

Juliette bent down and kissed first Lisa and then Nilly on the forehead. "Victor said you were two smart kids. And I can already see that he's right. Hurry up. Find him and come back."

They heard an angry shout from the hallway and rapid footsteps. The next second the door bulged into the room as if someone had just flung themselves against it. The door stopped bulging and they heard the creaking of the floorboards again, as if someone were taking another running start.

Lisa and Nilly took deep breaths and dived under the bubbles.

Then they were in a watery twilight where there was total silence.

Nilly could feel Lisa's hand holding on to his own as he concentrated. Naturally what he wanted to do most of all was travel back to the Moulin Rouge to that girl who had thought he was so cute, but you couldn't travel back to the same time and place more than once.

So instead he had to think about . . . about . . . where were they supposed to be going again? That's right, the Provence mountains. July . . . 3, 1969! More specifically Inn . . . Inn . . . what was that place that Juliette had said again? Darn it, it started with Inn! Inn . . . Inn . . .

Soon he couldn't hold his breath anymore.

Inn . . . Inn . . .

Must have air!

Inn . . . DARN IT!

Nilly stood up in the bath, gasping for air.

He was standing in a bath in the middle of a meadow full of colourful flowers. The sun was shining, bees were buzzing and birds were chirping all around him, and there were extremely tall mountains in every direction. At the other end of the meadow he saw a group of people sitting along the edge of a road in folding chairs waving French flags as they said cheers and clinked their wineglasses together and cheered on

bicyclists as they passed. It was a wonderfully beautiful summer's day out in the countryside. There were really only two things that concerned Nilly. One was that Lisa wasn't anywhere to be seen. The second was that a bull with horns the size of a Congolese tse-tse elephant's tusks was heading towards him at full speed.

Tour de France

THE BULL WAS the size of a small tractor but had a significantly faster maximum speed. Nilly realised that even if he ran as fast as his tiny legs could carry him, the bull was still going to overtake him. The ground beneath Nilly shook and he could hear the animal's terrible snorting. Bees and butterflies darted out of the bull's path in fear as Nilly raced through the flower-filled meadow that just seconds ago had seemed so idyllic and peaceful.

"Help," Nilly cried, but only very softly, because he knew that no one could help him, and that he should save his breath. He would need it if he was going to reach the fence before that beast of muscles and horns that was rapidly approaching him from behind. So, he very quietly called "help" one more time, before he accepted that no matter how much air he had left, he was not going to reach the fence first, that very soon he would be dangling from one of those massive barbecue skewer horns. Nilly prepared himself and then leaped up into the air, tucked his legs up, wrapped his arms round them, curled himself into a ball and screamed (without saving any breath): "Cannonball!"

With that, the tiny little boy disappeared. The bull stopped and stared down at the hillside that was covered with tall Bermuda grass, wild begonias, lily of the valley and other stuff that grows in French meadows and that the bull didn't even know the name of. The bull rummaged around in this salad with one of his horns, all the while realising that he was feeling even madder. Where the cow buttocks had that unbelievably irritating little chap gone?

Nilly wriggled through the grass, and he didn't stand up again until he was sure that he had crawled under the fence and past it. He turned towards the bull, who was still standing out there in the meadow sniffing the ground.

"Hey, yoo-hoo! Hey, Mr Beef, Medium Well!"

The bull raised his head and stared at Nilly, who put a thumb in each ear and wiggled his fingers and said "nyah, nyah" as he stuck out his tongue and blew a raspberry. The bull responded by blowing hot steaming air out of his splayed nostrils, positioning his legs on the ground and lowering his head. *What an insufferable, poorly behaved, rude young man,* he thought. Then he came barrelling. But he never made it to the red-haired boy. Seconds later, his enormous bull horns struck that idiotic bath that for some reason or other had suddenly appeared in the meadow. The bath was lifted up into the air, whirled round and then came down to land upside down so that all the water and soap bubbles ran out.

Nilly was going to laugh, but instead he stiffened. He dug around desperately in his wet pockets, but found only small things that started with *P*: a parking ticket, a plum stone and a sealed plastic bag of fartonaut powder. But not what he was looking for. Of course not, because Lisa was the one who had brought the jar of soap. All he had was an empty time-travelling bath! How was he ever going to get back?

Nilly stuck his index finger into his ear, rotated it round and pulled it out again. *Plop!* But even that didn't help. His brain didn't give him any answers.

He was doomed. So, Nilly wasn't laughing, not one bit.

But there were some other people who were.

Nilly turned to see where the laughter was coming from. And saw a short, thin man who was lying on his back in the grass with a blade of grass in the corner of his mouth. He was wearing a blue bicycling jersey with a number on it.

"Great sprint." The man laughed. "You ought to take up biking, kid."

"Thanks," Nilly said. And since he was a born optimist who also liked company and a good conversation, his outlook on the situation had already started to improve a bit.

"Do you know why bulls like that get so mad?" Nilly asked. "Did I do something to that sack of beef, or what?"

The guy said, "Red hair," and pointed at Nilly's head. "Bulls see red when they see red."

Nilly cocked his red-haired head to the side and looked at the man. "Um, how come you're speaking Norwegian?"

The man laughed again. "I'm speaking French, my friend. And so are you."

"I am?"

"You're certainly a very funny clown. What's your name?"

"Nilly. And I'm not a clown."

"You're not?" the man said. "You'll really have to excuse me, Nilly. I thought that was a clown nose."

Nilly reached up to feel his nose. He'd totally forgotten about the nose clip. Something was slowly starting to dawn on him. He pulled off the nose clip and tried: "And what's your name, man in the blue bicycling jersey?"

The man looked at him blankly. *"Keska too ah dee?"*

"Aha!" Nilly shouted triumphantly. It wasn't just dawning on him, it was broad daylight inside his head.

He understood everything. Well, almost everything. At any rate, he understood why he had understood what the cancan dancer had said, and what Juliette had meant when she'd said a lot would become clear to them if they kept the nose clips on. That was because these really were French nose clips. While you wore them you could understand French and you could speak French. What do you know, another ingenious Doctor Proctor invention!

Nilly was so excited that, as usual, he forgot all about his problems. He put his nose clip on and asked the man what his name was and why in the world he was lying here in the grass when all the other bicyclists he'd seen were riding as if their lives depended on it.

"My name's Eddy. And my bike has its third flat tyre of the day." He pointed over by the road where a racing bike was lying on its side. "I just couldn't take any-more. The finishing line is at the top of that mountain over there."

Eddy pointed again and Nilly had to bend his neck back to see the peak of the snow-capped mountain in front of them.

"What about you, Nilly?"

"I came from the future," Nilly said. "I think I came to the right time, but the wrong place. What year is it and what's the name of this place?"

Eddy laughed even louder. "Thank you, Nilly. At least you're cheering me up!"

"I'm not kidding."

"Well," Eddy said. "The year is 1969 and we're in Inndarnit. Where were you supposed to be?"

"Inndarnit?" Nilly mumbled, scratching his left side-burn. "I was supposed to be somewhere that started with 'Inn' but I forgot the rest. Lisa must be there now, you know?"

"Lisa?"

"Yeah, we're supposed to find Doctor Proctor. Maybe she's already found him, and now they're just waiting for me to show up. It's actually totally crucial that I find them. Without them I'm going to be stuck here in 1969."

"That doesn't sound good," Eddy said. He took a little drink from his water bottle and passed it to Nilly. "1969 really sucks."

"Oh?" Nilly asked.

"Nothing but flat tyres in every single race," Eddy said. "Just as bad as 1815 was for Napoléon."

"1815? Napoléon?"

"Don't you remember?"

Nilly thought about it. "I don't think I was born then."

"From history class, silly! June eighteenth, 1815. That was when Napoléon led his troops . . ."

". . . across the Alps?" Nilly tried.

"No," Eddy said, waving away a bumblebee. "That was when he took a licking in the Battle of Waterloo. And I know that quite well, because Waterloo is just a few minutes of Eddy-biking from my dad's bike shop in Belgium. Totally flat country. You know what? Now that I'm giving up biking, I think I'll go home and see if I can get a job there."

"Good thinking," Nilly said, taking a drink from the water bottle. "Because, really, what's the point of biking up and down all these mountains? They're way too big."

"The point?" Eddy was staring at Nilly as if Nilly had reminded him of something he'd forgotten.

"Yeah," Nilly said, gulping down more water. All this time travel had made him unusually thirsty.

"This is the Tour de France," Eddy said. "Whoever wins this mountain stage wins money, gets kissed on the cheek by cute girls and will be interviewed on TV while everyone in France watches."

Nilly thought about that, and began to see that perhaps there was some point to it after all. Especially the part about being kissed by cute girls. And being seen on TV by everyone in France couldn't really hurt either . . .

"Hey!" Nilly cried. "Did you just say *everyone in France*?"

"Absolutely everyone," Eddy said. "Every TV in France is on for the Tour de France. You can't not see it."

"Even if you don't have a TV at home?"

"They set up TVs in every single café, restaurant and country shop. *Merde!* You've got to stop making me talk about this stuff, Nilly! Now I just want to fling myself back on my bike and win this darned race!"

"That's exactly what you're going to do!" Nilly shouted. Then he ran over to Eddy and pulled him up onto his feet.

"What?" Eddy asked.

"First I'm going to help you fix your tyre and then we're going to fart our way up to the top of this mountain and be interviewed on TV."

"We?" Eddy asked as Nilly pushed him towards his bike.

"Yup. Because I'm going to sit in on the interview. And I'll say that Lisa and Doctor Proctor have to come and pick me up, so we can return to our own time."

"You sure say a lot of funny-sounding things," Eddy mumbled and took out his puncture kit. "But at least you've given me back my desire to win."

TWO MINUTES LATER, two cud-chewing sheep raised their heads as a bike passed them on the road just outside their fence.

"Did you see that?" the one cud-chewing sheep said to the other. "Two people on one bike. Isn't that cheating?"

The other sheep blinked his eyes sleepily. "Baaa, why? It makes the bike even heavier when you're going uphill. Besides, they're dead last."

"That's not the point," the one sheep said. "Is it *allowed*?"

The other chewed his cud for a bit while he contemplated this.

"No idea," he finally said. "I'm a sheep, you know? We don't know that kind of thing."

* * *

EDDY STOOD ON his pedals and pushed as hard as he could. Not just because standing on the pedals helped him go faster, but because his seat was occupied by a red-haired little guy with a nose clip who was screaming into his ear:

"Come on, Eddy! Faster, Eddy! You're the best, Eddy!"

And when Eddy tried to ease up on the pace a little:

"Pull yourself together, Eddy! Do you want a licking, Eddy? Do you want this to be your Waterloo, Eddy? Do you want to be a full-time tyre-fixer, Eddy? You can do more! It feels gooood to be tired!"

And, truth be told, it was helping. Soon they started overtaking cyclists who stared open-mouthed at the strange two-man team with the little boy screaming:

"Push, Eddy! The other cyclists are even tireder! Think about the girls waiting at the top, Eddy. They have soft lips. Sooooooft lips, Eddy. Faster, faster, otherwise I'm going to give you a noogie! And we're not talking about a little love noogie, we're talking about a massive, Yeti noogie!"

Eddy, who wasn't really sure what a noogie was, but didn't particularly want to find out either, pushed. His tongue was hanging out of his mouth, and his breath had started making a strange, rasping sound. But they were still passing cyclist after cyclist and had made it quite a way up the mountain, to where there were still patches of snow in the shadows. Even though Nilly's clothes had dried in the sunshine, he was now so cold that his teeth chattered as he chanted his mixture of encouragement and threats. Until a wheezing Eddy interrupted him:

"I can't do it . . ."

"What?" Nilly yelled through his chattering teeth. "Do you want a n-n-noogie, you B-B-Belgian waffle!"

"The finishing line is too close . . ." wheezed Eddy. "We won't be able to pass everyone."

"Nonsense," Nilly said. "I said we would fart up this mountain and when Nilly says we'll fart up a mountain, you'd darn well better—"

"Fart all you want . . ." Eddy groaned. His tongue was hanging down to the handlebars and the bike had started wobbling ominously. "Look at how steep this is."

Nilly looked. The road was so steep that it looked like a wall. And way, way up ahead, high, high above them he saw the yellow jersey of the guy in front.

"Hm," Nilly said.

"Hm what?" Eddy wheezed.

"I'm going to fart." Nilly stuck his hand in his pocket and fished out a plastic bag, which he resolutely opened and then poured the contents into his mouth.

"What was that?" Eddy asked.

"That was a little carry-on item starting with *P*," Nilly said, and burped. "Hold on tight. Six – five – four – three – two . . ."

"Hold on . . . ?"

Eddy didn't have a chance to say anything else. There was a bang so loud that it felt like the earwax was being pushed into his ears and his eyes bulged out of his head. And then there was a roar, like from a speeding rocket engine. The reason he thought of a rocket engine specifically was that they were rushing up the mountain sort of like – well, actually, exactly like – a rocket!

"Yippee!" Nilly cheered in his ear.

"Yippee!" Eddy cheered as they passed the cyclists ahead of them and had only the one in the yellow jersey left to overtake. But there was the finishing line! And the guy in the yellow jersey had only a few metres to go.

"Give it all you got, Nilly!" Eddy yelled, steering the bike as best he could so they wouldn't run right off the side of the mountain. "Full fart steam ahead! Otherwise it's noogie-time for you!"

"I'm trying," groaned Nilly, who was very red in the face.

"Faster, Nilly, we're not going to make it! Think about those soooooft lips!"

And Nilly thought. He thought that if they didn't manage this, he would probably never get to see Lisa or Doctor Proctor again. This thought made his intestines give one final effort and he pressed out a little more wind so they shot ahead with a little more speed. The spectators watching would talk about it for years afterwards – that they had been witness to the fantastic sprint in the Provence mountains at the 1969 Tour de France, when the legendary Eddy and his strange red-haired passenger, whose name no one could remember, had flown towards the finishing line as if they had a jet engine on their bike. Some even claimed that the bicycle had lifted off from the ground. Yes, a few even imagined that a strange white smoke had trailed from the seat of the trousers of the little boy on the bike seat. Even so, it had appeared hopeless, up until the final metres when they had managed to increase their speed a tiny bit more and at the finishing line they had beaten the yellow jersey by a gumillionth of a millimetre. It was the first victory for Eddy, who would go on to became the world-famous Eddy who would win bike races around the world, but who in his memoirs would say that it had been that win in Provence that had made him believe in himself and stick with cycling.

But all that was in the future (or the past, depending on how you looked at it). Right now (or then) Eddy and Nilly were revelling in their win. They were both lifted off the bike and carried by the cheering crowd over to the winner's platform, where they were given a medal and each given a teddy bear and kissed on the cheek by soooft lips. Then someone thrust a microphone in their faces and Nilly immediately pushed his way forward.

"Hello," he said. "Is this TV?"

"Yes," said the woman behind the microphone. "Can you tell the French people who you actually are?"

"Certainly," Nilly said. "Where's the camera?"

"Over there," the woman said, and pointed towards an enormous camera set up in the back of a nearby truck behind her.

Nilly looked directly into the camera and stood up straight.

"Hi there, people of France," he said. "I'm Nilly, and I think you should make a note of that name.

 Especially if there's anyone out there named Lisa or Doctor Proctor, I think they should pay attention now. I – Nilly, that is – am coming to you live from the top of a mountain named—"

"We know the name of the mountain," the woman with the microphone said impatiently. "You entered the world of cycle racing like a comet, *Muhsyuh* Nilly, but have you come to stay?"

"No," Nilly said. "Actually, I would like to get out of here as soon as possible, so if Lisa and Doctor Proctor could come and pick me up, I'll be waiting at the top of . . . What mountain is this, actually?"

"Moe Bla," Eddy whispered into his ear.

"Moe Bla!" Nilly shouted. "To be precise, I'll be at the . . ."

"Hôtel Moe Bla," Eddy whispered.

"Hôtel Moe Bla!" Nilly yelled.

"My buddy and I will be staying in the tower suite," Eddy told the camera. "The winner always gets the tower suite. Hurry, Lisa and Doctor Proctor!"

WHEN THE INTERVIEW was over, they were whisked off for massages and a wonderful hot bath in the tower suite. A tailor came up to the room, took Nilly's measurements, and shook his head, laughing, before disappearing again. When he returned a few hours later, he brought a suit and shirt and shoes that Nilly was told to wear to the victory dinner.

"Cool!" Nilly cried as he looked at himself in the mirror. "Will there be cancan dancing?"

Eddy laughed and shook his head exactly the way the tailor had. "The next stage starts tomorrow at eight a.m. sharp. I'm going to eat four French fries and then turn in for the night."

"Party pooper!" Nilly complained, tap dancing in his new patent leather shoes so they clicked on the marble floor. "Let's get this party started!"

The victory dinner was being held in the restaurant of the Hôtel Moe Bla. There were lots of people in fancy party clothes who wanted to shake Nilly's hand, but there was no cancan content as far as he could tell. Some of the other cyclists came over to Nilly and asked him in a whisper about the powder they'd seen him take, wondering if they could buy some from him. They snarled "cheater!" when Nilly shook his head. Actually the whole thing was pretty boring. Nilly's head was already nodding as he started dozing off during the first course. He eventually slid down in his seat, unnoticed, and disappeared out of sight under the edge of the table. Eddy discovered the sleeping Nilly. After three attempts to wake him, he slung Nilly over his shoulder and carried him up the stairs to the tower suite. There he placed Nilly in the bigger of the two beds and crawled into the smaller one himself. Then he yawned twice and turned off the lights.

NILLY WOKE UP and opened his eyes. A strip of sunlight was coming in through a gap in the curtains in the tower suite and shining right on his freckled face. He stretched and discovered that someone had put a teeny tiny yellow jersey on his nightstand. It said TOUR DE FRANCE 1969 on it and next to it there was a note that said:

Good morning, Nilly! Thanks for your help. I didn't want to wake you, so by

the time you read this we'll already be
out riding the next stage. I hope Lisa
and Doctor Proctor come soon.

Your friend always,
Eddy

Nilly stretched, feeling fit, like he was in great shape, but also, truth be told, like he could do with a little more sleep. He thought about it a little, yawned and closed his eyes again. And then he thought about breakfast. The second he thought about that, he heard the door open quietly and smelled the familiar scent of food. He smiled and dreamed of what types of delicious dishes were being wheeled in to him now. Yes, he didn't even need to open his eyes to tell that it was a wheeled cart. He could hear the wheels squeaking.

The squeaking wheels . . .

Nilly's eyes shot open and he stared at the ceiling. He inhaled the scent of food again. It wasn't bacon and eggs. It was . . . rotten meat and stinky socks.

He jumped in bed as the door slammed shut and the key turned. There, right in front of him, stood a tall person in a long, black trench coat with a wooden leg sticking out at the bottom.

The person's red made-up lips were stretched into an unusually big grin that revealed those sharp, chalk-white teeth. In her hand she was holding a long-barrelled pistol that looked like it had been stolen from a museum. The person's voice was as hoarse as a desert wind:

"Good morning, Nilly. Where is he? Where's Doctor Proctor?"

"R-r-r . . ." Nilly said. "Ra-ra-ra . . ."

There was no doubt about it. His stutter was back.

The Bridge in Provence

LISA STOOD THERE in the bath with water dripping from her clothes, blinking the soap bubbles out of her eyelashes. She looked around. The first thing she discovered was that she was surrounded by tall, gloomy mountains that blocked out the sun. The second was that the bath was on a grassy ledge. The third was that right in front of her was a bridge, a steel bridge that was sooty and grey from age. The fourth was that she was completely alone. In other words, Nilly was nowhere to be seen.

"Nilly!" Lisa yelled.

"Nilly!" the echo replied, first from the side of one mountain, then another and then another.

She hopped out of the bath and walked over to the edge of the rocky ledge. A deep chasm plunged down between mountains, below her and the bridge.

"Nilly!"

"Nilly! Nilly! Nilly. . ." The echoes faded away.

"Hi!"

The "hi" had come from the bridge. Lisa shaded her eyes and felt a sense of hope well up in her when she glimpsed someone standing on the road by the end of the bridge waving to her. Maybe that was Nilly? Or Doctor Proctor?

"Hi!" Lisa yelled, waving back and starting to wade

through grass down the hillside, heading over towards the road. As she walked, she heard something, the drone of an engine approaching. And she heard that the voice up ahead yelled something back. She stopped so she could hear better:

"Hurry up! They're coming!"

The voice didn't sound like Nilly's or Doctor Proctor's. It was a girl's voice. Lisa heard the drone of the engine getting louder and instinctively understood that she should do what the girl said. So she did. She hurried. Lisa ran as fast as she could, as the sound of the engine got louder and louder. When Lisa reached the end of the bridge, she saw that the person was a girl a little younger than herself, with dark hair, brown eyes and a red poncho. The girl grabbed Lisa's hand and pulled her down to hide in the ditch alongside the road just as a motorcycle came around the corner.

And it was a motorcycle Lisa recognised right away.

It had a sidecar, and the driver was tall and thin and wearing motorcycle goggles, a leather helmet and a most unusually long wool scarf that stretched straight out behind him and disappeared round the corner. And then, wouldn't you know, the end of the scarf came round the corner too. A woman was hanging on to it, being pulled as if she was on water skis. The soles of her shoes were emitting black smoke, like from burning rubber. Lisa opened her mouth in disbelief. She knew what was going to happen!

And that was exactly what *did* happen too. Just much faster than Lisa had pictured it when Juliette had described it: the woman slid along the edge of the road, the scarf coiled round the sign post before the bridge, and partway across the bridge, the driver was yanked off his motorcycle as the scarf tightened round his neck. Meanwhile, the woman was spinning round the post in tighter and tighter circles. Sparks sprayed out from around the motorcycle as it slid over the

bridge until it finally stopped and silence once again settled between the mountains.

"Juliette!" Lisa yelled to the woman, who had finally released the scarf and was obviously very dizzy after her carousel ride because she staggered out onto the bridge without paying any attention to Lisa's yell.

"Juliette!" Lisa yelled and wanted to run after her. But the girl in the poncho held her back.

"He said we were supposed to stay here," she said.

"Who said?" Lisa yelled, trying to pull herself free.

"Doctor Proctor," the girl said.

Lisa stiffened. "Doctor Proctor was here?"

"Yes," the girl said. "He said that we had to let what happened happen. That trying to stop it could ruin his other plans. Duck, here come the hippos!"

It wasn't until she heard the word "hippo" that Lisa noticed the sound of another engine and knew that they were coming, just as Juliette had described. And sure enough, the black limousine came round the corner. It drove cautiously onto the bridge, which was only just barely wide enough.

Lisa remained crouched and watched the woman out on the bridge pull the man onto his feet.

"He's going to get on his motorcycle soon and drive off towards Italy," Lisa whispered. "And she'll turn herself over to the hippos, who will take her back to Claude Cliché in Paris. Whom she'll have to marry."

"I know," the girl said, and as Lisa stared at her, wondering how she knew all that, the girl continued: "The professor told me. What time did you come from?"

"The same as Doctor Proctor. How did you know that I'd time-travelled?"

"I saw the bath. What's your name?"

"Lisa. Lisa Pedersen. I'm here to find Doctor Proctor. Did you time-travel here too?"

The girl laughed and shook her head. "I'm just from here and now. My name's Anna. Anna Showli."

"How funny," Lisa said. "My best friend's name is Anna, too. She lives in Sarpsborg. In Norway. My parents think I'm there visiting her now." Lisa felt her eyes suddenly well up at the thought of her mother and father.

Anna smiled and patted Lisa comfortingly on the cheek, even though Anna looked like she must be at least a year younger than Lisa. On the other hand, if Lisa ever got back to her own time and met Anna then, Anna would be at least as old as her mother.

"Are you alone?" Anna asked.

"So it would seem," Lisa said. "I'm guessing Nilly forgot where we were going. Occasionally he has trouble concentrating."

The motorcycle out on the bridge started up and drove away.

"Hey!" Lisa yelled, standing up. "Doctor Proctor! Don't go!"

"Shh," Anna said, pulling Lisa back down. "That's

the young Doctor Proctor. He wouldn't have had any idea what you were talking about."

"Huh?" Lisa said. "What happened to the old Doctor Proctor, then?"

Anna sighed. "He left again."

"But he was here? You met him?"

Anna nodded. "He strolled into Innebrède this morning, wet as a pair of swimming trunks. He came over to me, because the Trann cousins had tossed me into Innebrède Creek yet again."

"The Trann cousins?"

"These two awful boys who live down at the bottom of my street. They had knocked over my bike, dumped out my backpack and filled my pockets with nails. They're training to be hippos like their fathers, you see."

"I see," Lisa sighed.

"Well, I guess his crazy appearance scared them. At least that's what I assume. Plus, he was shouting at them in a foreign language and shaking his fist. The Trann boys ran off, but yelled to me that they were going to go get their fathers. Then the professor helped me gather my books and school things. And when he saw that I had a big magic marker, he asked if he could borrow it to write a message on the wall at the petrol station."

"A message?"

"Yeah. He wanted to warn himself, he said. He was going to write a note telling himself not to stop there, to keep going until he got to Italy. He told me the whole story."

"And you believed him?" Lisa asked, surprised.

"No, no," Anna laughed. "I thought he was a nice, but very crazy, professor. Even though he showed me the bath that he claimed he could travel through time in. It was in with all the junk cars in the Hippo's scrap-metal yard. Then I heard the bell ringing at school off in the distance and explained to him how to get to the petrol station without running into the Trann fathers. Then I ran off so I wouldn't be late for school."

"I see," Lisa said. "So, why aren't you at school now?"

"I never made it that far. When I came round the corner, the Trann fathers were there waiting for me. They shook me and asked me who he was, that crazy foreigner who'd threatened those dear, sweet boys of theirs. I was so scared, I told them everything. They made such strange faces when I told them about the young professor who was running away with Juliette Margarine by motorcycle. They said something about how that must be the guy their boss, Mr Cliché, was looking for. They asked if I knew where the foreigner was, but I pretended I didn't know. Then they let me go and started discussing something between themselves. They agreed to warn the other hippos in the village to keep a lookout for suspicious foreigners. And decided it probably made sense to give the petrol station a heads-up since that was usually where any foreigners coming to Innebrède went. Then they jumped into their limousine and drove away."

"What did you do?"

"I realised right away that maybe there was something to the professor's story after all. So, I ran as fast as I could in the same direction I'd told the professor to go. *Moan dyoo*, how I ran! Luckily I found him hiding across from the petrol station. I told him what had happened. We watched from his hiding place and saw that the limousine was there already and that the Trann fathers were talking to the two hippos who work at the petrol station."

"That explains why they were so suspicious when Proctor and Juliette stopped for petrol," Lisa said.

Anna's eyes welled up. "It's all my fault, isn't it?"

"Not at all," Lisa said, and now she was the one patting Anna's cheek. "There's no way you could have known that Doctor Proctor isn't completely insane. To tell the truth, sometimes I wonder myself. . ."

Anna dried away her tears. "The professor said that his plan had failed, that he had to come up with something else."

"Did he say what?" Lisa asked.

"He said you only get one chance to change something in history, so now he had to go to another time and change something there."

"Where?" Lisa asked. "Where?"

"He said he had a brilliant idea."

"What idea?" Lisa shouted.

"Duck!" Anna said.

The wide limousine had backed up off the bridge and was now turning round right in front of them. Lisa cautiously peeked over the edge of the ditch and caught a glimpse of a pale face inside, behind the dark tinted windows. It was Juliette. Then the limo accelerated and disappeared in a cloud of dust.

"What kind of idea?" Lisa repeated, coughing.

"The professor wanted to travel back in time to see the engineer who designed this bridge in front of us. To before he made it. To get him to change the drawings."

"Change the bridge? Why?"

"Because the limousine that the hippos use is exactly as wide as the American tanks that rolled across the bridge here to liberate France from Hitler during World War Two. You said it yourself that the limousine only just barely fitted onto the bridge, right?"

"Yeah," Lisa said.

"Well, the professor said that if he could just get the engineer to draw the bridge a *tiny bit* narrower in 1888, then the limousine wouldn't fit and the hippos would have to give up and stop chasing him and Juliette. And they could just chug along on their way. And live happily ever after . . ."

"Brilliant!" Lisa exclaimed. "How clever! But . . . but how did he know who the engineer was and what year he drew the plans?"

"Simple! It's on that sign right there." Anna pointed and the two girls got up out of the ditch and went over to the sign that the scarf had been caught on.

"Designed by engineer Gustave Eiffel in 1888," Lisa read. "Completed in 1894. Wait! Eiffel? Isn't he the guy who designed—"

"Yup," Anna said. "He's the one who designed the Eiffel Tower. And there you have it. The professor decided to go visit Gustave Eiffel in 1888. So he said goodbye, sank down into the bath and – voilà! – he was gone! I even felt around in the bath for him. And that's when I realised that he might not be that crazy after all. So, instead of riding my bike home, I came here to see if what the professor had described to me would happen, would really happen. And it did."

Anna suddenly looked sad again. "The professor's poor girlfriend, though. Imagine having to marry that scoundrel Claude Cliché."

Suddenly she punched the palm of her hand. "I can't believe none of those cowardly judges in Paris have had the courage to throw the book at that hoodlum!

It makes me so mad that everyone just does what he says."

"Unfortunately there's nothing we can do about guys like Cliché," Lisa said. "But now I have to go and find the doctor. I have the soap he needs." Lisa patted her jacket pocket.

Anna followed Lisa, who had had a running start. She had jumped over the ditch and was now running through the grass back towards the ledge where the time-travelling bath was. When they got there, Lisa was relieved to see that there were still bubbles.

"Thank you for all your help, Anna," Lisa said, jumping in. "You'll see. What you've done will end up helping to save the professor after all."

"I hope so," Anna said. "But I hope you're not right about the other thing."

"What other thing?"

"That there's nothing we can do to stop guys like Claude Cliché."

"You should try," Lisa said. "Good luck, Anna Showli."

"Good luck to you too, Lisa Pedersen. Say hi to the professor from me when you see him."

"I will, I promise." Lisa went to plug her nose with her fingers, but discovered that she was still wearing the blue nose clip.

"Hey, the professor said one other thing," Anna said. "That I should be careful if his old assistant showed up. His assistant is apparently able to track people by reading the soap residue and can follow people no matter what time they travel to."

"Yeah, that was my understanding too, that his assistant was kind of a shady guy," Lisa said. "Okay, bye!"

"But . . ." Anna started.

But it was too late, because Lisa had already disappeared into the bubbles.

". . . his assistant wasn't a guy," Anna continued,

mumbling. "The professor told me it was a woman. A very unusual woman . . ."

Meanwhile, under the water, Lisa was concentrating on Gustave Eiffel's office and a date in 1888. But which date? She chose the first one she thought of, May 17, Norwegian Independence Day. That's as good as any other date, right?

FROM HIS BED in the tower suite at the Hôtel Moe Bla, Nilly was staring into the muzzle of an old-fashioned pistol. And thinking that he would much rather be staring at a plate of bacon and eggs. Not just because he was awfully hungry, but because pistol muzzles are unpleasant things to stare at. A bullet could come shooting out at any time.

"Feet on the floor, don your duds and ten hut," the woman behind the pistol commanded.

"Wh-wh-why?" Nilly stuttered, pulling the covers up to his chin.

"Because you're going to help me find the man who ruined my life."

"Wh-wh-who's that?"

Raspa's eyes glowed with hatred as she whispered hoarsely, "Doctor Proctor, of course."

Raspa's Story

LET'S REWIND FOR five seconds and then pick up again where we left off.

"You're going to help me find the man who ruined my life," Raspa snarled with a pistol aimed at the bed in which our hero, Nilly, was lying with the covers pulled up to his chin.

"Wh-wh-who's that?" whispered Nilly, who maybe wasn't looking quite as heroic as we might have wished.

Raspa's eyes seethed with hatred as she whispered hoarsely, "Doctor Proctor, of course."

Nilly swallowed and asked, "C-c-couldn't I just tell him you said hello when I see him next?"

"GET UP!" Raspa bellowed, the pistol in her hand shaking.

"Okay, okay!" Nilly said, tossing off the covers and hopping out of bed onto the floor. "You don't need to yell like that. What do you want with that shabby old professor, anyway?"

"Not much," Raspa said, sinking down into an armchair as she watched Nilly get dressed. "I just want what's mine."

"And that is . . . ?"

"Elementary, my dear young sailor. The drawings for the time-travelling bath."

"Yours? Didn't Doctor Proctor discover——"

"But I was the one who invented the time soap bath bombs!" Raspa growled, white drops of spit spraying from her mouth. "And then that idiot betrayed me! Messed everything up by falling in love with this Juliette woman. Just her name makes my mouth taste like rancid butter. He ruined everything!"

"So you were . . . you were . . ."

"Yes, I was his assistant. But I was at least as smart as he was!"

"And now you want to find him so that you can steal his part of the invention."

"Hurry up!"

Nilly discovered that he'd put his shoes on before his trousers and had to start all over again. "Why should I help you find the professor if you're just going to steal from him?"

Raspa waved the pistol.

"Oh yeah, right," Nilly mumbled as he pulled on his

trousers. "What's going to happen to us after you get your claws on the drawings?"

"If I were you," Raspa said, scratching the side of her nose with the pistol, "I would try not to think about that. Concentrate instead on where the professor might be."

"I have no idea," Nilly said. "So sue me, but I really have no idea."

"People can't be bothered to sue dead dwarves," Raspa said, waving the pistol.

"Well, as a matter of fact, I do remember that it starts with 'In'," Nilly said hurriedly. "And that could really be so many places. India, for example. Or Indonesia. The Incan Empire. Inishshark Island in Ireland . . ."

"Stop!" Raspa snarled, raising the pistol. "You're obviously no help, you snotty-nosed brat. So, farewell . . ."

Nilly could see her long, crooked index finger curling round the trigger and starting to pull back on it.

"Wait!" he screamed. "I just thought of it!"

Raspa squinted at him in suspicion without lowering her pistol. "Oh, did you now?"

"Yes, yes, yes!" Nilly said, nodding so energetically that his fringe painted red streaks through the air.

"Well? Where?"

"We need a time-travelling bath to get there," Nilly said. He ran over to the bathroom and pulled open the door. "Can you set up this bath?"

"No, you idiot!" Raspa railed. "Not without Proctor's drawings. We have to go back to the bath in that blasted meadow. I landed right on my head when I arrived . . ." Raspa complained, rubbing her forehead, and only now did Nilly notice a blue lump right at her hairline.

"You came here in the same bath as me?"

"Of course," Raspa mumbled.

"How?"

"Enough talk. Time to ship out," Raspa said, and

then opened the door and waved Nilly out into the hallway with her pistol.

Nilly gasped in disbelief. "*Before* breakfast? Are you aware that breakfast is *included* in the price at this hotel? That it's *complimentary*?"

"NOW!"

Nilly shrugged.

"All right," he said innocently. Precisely as innocently as someone who's just had a not-altogether-so-innocent idea. Because Nilly had actually just figured out that they had to get out onto the street so he could sneak off and, thanks to his small stature, disappear in the crowd.

"Come on," he said, strutting out. Raspa followed, sticking the pistol into her coat pocket as they went down the stairs. When they came out onto the street, Nilly looked around in confusion. The clouds had rolled in overnight and now it felt like it was about to start raining. But that's not what was confusing him.

"Hey, where did everybody go? There was a huge crowd out here yesterday."

"They followed the cycling circus to its next stop," Raspa said, peering down the empty street. "Oh, too bad. Did that ruin your plan to sneak away and, thanks to your small stature, disappear in the crowd?"

Nilly didn't respond. *What, could she read minds too?*

Raspa laughed. "Come on, pipsqueak, hop up onto my back."

"Your back?"

"Do you see a taxi or something instead?"

"No . . ." Nilly said, sounding reluctant.

Raspa bent down. "Hop on. Let's get down off this damned mountain before it starts pouring."

Nilly hesitated, but did as she asked. Once Raspa was sure that he was holding on tight enough, she kicked off. The ungreased wheels at the bottom of her wooden leg squealed. They rumbled over the asphalt as they passed under the finishing line that was still up. They started speeding up.

"Hold on tight," Raspa said over her shoulder. "Full steam ahead."

She hunched over. Thunder rumbled in the distance and the wind beat against Nilly's face as they whooshed down the same desolate, extremely steep mountain road that Eddy and Nilly had struggled their way up the day before. Raspa leaned into the turns, causing her rubber roller-skate wheels to shriek.

And Nilly, since he was Nilly, totally forgot what an awkward situation he was in and cheered happily, "Yippee! Faster! Faster!"

He got what he wanted. Ultimately they were moving so fast that the air pressure made their cheeks flap, flipped their eyelids back and flattened their noses against their faces. Nilly suddenly stopped shouting when his tongue disappeared down his throat and he had to shut his mouth so he could cough it back up again.

* * *

TWO SHEEP WERE standing next to each other watching the – to put it mildly – peculiar woman with the boy on her back, who was the same boy who had sped past them the day before going the other way.

"Haven't we seen that red-headed chap before?" one of the cud-chewing sheep said to the other.

"No idea," the second cud-chewer replied to the first. "We're sheep, you know. We don't remember stuff like that."

RASPA AND NILLY were almost horizontal by the time they reached the final curve before the road flattened out and Nilly spotted the flower-filled meadow. And the feet of the upside-down bath.

That very instant, the clouds opened up. And boy did it rain! It was as if the biggest raindrops in the whole world had gathered over this specific meadow to hold the world championships in The Last Raindrop to the Ground Is a Rotten Egg.

"Perfect," Raspa shouted, hopping over the fence and starting to limp through the grass towards the bath.

"Pe-rf-ect?" Nilly asked, as he bumped up and down

on Raspa's back and felt the rain streaming down the back of his neck and in under his jersey.

Raspa was heading straight for the bath. She wiggled so Nilly fell off and tumbled down into the grass. Then she grabbed one of the bath's feet. "Help me right her so we can launch."

Nilly stood up and did as she asked. They turned the bath over so it was right side up and watched the rain hammering against the enamelled bottom. Raspa took out a jar, which she opened and poured from. A familiar strawberry-red powder sprinkled down into the bath, where the rain frothed up the soap, which starting forming bubbles right away.

"Now we just have to wait until the bath is full," she said, climbing in and sitting down at one end. Nilly climbed in and sat down at the other end.

"So how did you find us, anyway?" Nilly asked.

"Easy," Raspa said. "When I noticed that you came in with a stamp from 1888 that looked brand-new and also had traces of white soap around the edges, I had a suspicion. When it tasted like strawberries, too, I knew that that could only mean one thing: that Proctor had got his time-travelling bath to work. And you're not exactly good at keeping a secret, sailor. When you said you were going to Paris, I realised that you would lead me right to him."

"You followed us."

"I did. I stood watch outside the Hôtel Frainche-Fraille, and when I saw the little girl come back with that awful woman—"

"Juliette Margarine, awful?"

"Don't say that name!" Raspa snarled. "They went up to the room, and I knew that you must be up there, all four of you. So I knocked—"

"Oh, we thought that was the hippos," said Nilly, who could feel that the water level had risen a little, but even a downpour takes a while to fill a whole time-travelling bath.

"I was trying to knock down the door, but I had to give up. So I ran downstairs, to that little wimp at the reception desk, and politely asked for the room key."

"And he just gave it to you?" Nilly asked in disbelief.

"I asked *very* politely," Raspa said. "Plus, I was pointing the pistol at him."

"Oh," Nilly said. "Good thinking."

"But when I got into the room, it was empty," Raspa sighed. "Proctor wasn't there and neither was anyone else. I turned the place upside down. Not a living soul. Just a stupid seven-legged spider. Seven legs! If it weren't for the fact that they don't exist, you might have thought it was a seven-legged Peruvian sucking spider."

Nilly didn't respond.

"So I realised you'd escaped in the time-travelling bath, and I started reading the tracks left in the soap . . ."

"Can you really track people from the soap?"

"Of course," Raspa sniffed in irritation. The rain

was making her make-up run in black rivulets. "I'm the one who invented the soap, I know *everything* there is to know about it. The only problem was that there were multiple tracks. You'd all gone to different places, so I had to pick one of them. And that led me here. I walked over to that café over there and saw you on TV. Nice of you to say exactly where you were. And now you're going to be just as nice and lead me to wherever Proctor went. Let's go now, and no funny business. I'll just follow your tracks no matter where you go. Keep that in mind."

"But I—" Nilly began, sticking his index finger in his ear and twisting it round.

"It's time to go!" Raspa said, raising her pistol. Water dripped from the end of the barrel. "Take your finger out of your ear!"

There was another thunderclap, close enough to make the ground shake this time.

"Oooooookay," Nilly said with a shudder, and a

little *plop!* was heard as his index finger quickly exited his ear.

But it hadn't been the pistol that had made Nilly shudder. Or the cold water. Or the crazy plan that had just formed in his head with a *plop!* Nilly had shuddered because he'd just discovered that the thunder that was making the ground shake wasn't coming from the sky. But from something heavy that was charging towards them from behind Raspa. An enormous, black, exceptionally enraged bull.

"It's time to go," Nilly said, diving down into the bath.

He held his breath and concentrated. He concentrated on what Eddy had told him, because that was the crux of his new plan. He wasn't sure if it was a particularly *good* plan, but nevertheless he concentrated on a place right next to a bike-repair shop in Belgium. The place was called Waterloo. The date was June 18, 1815. Napoléon Bonaparte's bedroom, Nilly thought.

When he surfaced again at first he thought he'd messed up somehow, because he could still hear thunder. But then he discovered that it was almost totally dark and that he was in a tent. And he realised that the thunder didn't have anything to do with lightning or bulls. It was a deep, rumbling snore. It was night-time and Nilly was at the Battle of Waterloo, the most famous military battle in history. And Nilly knew enough history to know that he'd ended up on the side that was going to lose, that was going to be trounced, smashed to smithereens and sent running for their lives.

To summarise: Nilly no longer had any doubt. He was now quite certain that this had *not* been a good plan.

Waterloo

NILLY BLINKED IN the darkness. He was wet, he was scared and he still hadn't had any breakfast. Basically this day was not starting out the way he would have liked. And now, on top of all that, it was also going to be the worst day in French military history, the day they would be decimated by the wretched English and the at least equally wretched Germans.

Nilly's eyes adjusted to the darkness and he saw that the thunderous snoring was coming from a bed located in the centre of the tent. Next to the bed there was a chair with a uniform draped neatly over its back. Nilly shivered. Of course the uniform would be way too big, but at least it would be dry. He quietly slipped out of the bath and sneaked over to the chair, pulling off his wet clothes as he went. He put on the uniform, and – what the heck was this? – it actually fitted him! Nilly looked down at the bed, at the man lying on his back and snoring with his mouth wide open. Could this really be the great general and dictator, Napoléon Bonaparte? Why, this guy was just as tiny as Nilly! But, no time to think about that now. Nilly hurriedly buttoned all the shiny buttons on the uniform, buckled the belt with the shiny sabre that only just barely dragged on the ground, and grabbed the strange, three-cornered hat that was sitting on the seat of the chair. How would you even begin to figure out which is the front and which is the back of a hat like this? No time to think about that either, because it wasn't going to take Raspa long to read the soap and be here. Nilly put the hat on his head and pulled the jar of fartonaut powder out of the pocket of his wet trousers. And then spun round because he heard someone sneeze behind him. But it wasn't Raspa. The sneeze had come from outside the tent.

"Bless you," he heard a voice outside the tent say.

Nilly exhaled in relief, opened the bag of fartonaut powder, held it carefully over the snoring general's gaping mouth and poured. But right then the little man exhaled, making a long, wheezing sound and blowing the powder right back in Nilly's face. Nilly's eyes started watering and he got powder in his nose and, before he could stop himself, he sneezed. When he opened his eyes again, he saw that the general's whole face was covered with splotches of wet fartonaut powder. Nilly held his breath.

"And bless you to you too," he heard another voice outside the tent say.

Then everything was once again drowned out by one of Napoléon's rattling breathing-in snores, and Nilly hurriedly used the opportunity to pour more powder into his mouth. Suddenly, the breathing-in snore stopped and Nilly's heart did too. For a few seconds the only thing you could hear was a cricket chirping outside. Then the general's breathing-in snore started again and so did Nilly's heart. Now it was just a question of waiting and counting down. Nilly moved to the back of the tent, closed his eyes, covered his ears with his hands and counted down to himself.

Six – five – four – three – two – one . . .

KABOOOM!!!

TWO OF NAPOLÉON Bonaparte's personal body-guards were standing just outside the tent. Both were half-asleep and both were half-deaf from all the cannon firings their ears had had to withstand throughout their long careers as soldiers. But both of them jumped to attention when they heard the giant *boom*.

"What in the world was that?" one of the guards asked, taking his rifle off his shoulder and exhaling nervously through his handlebar moustache.

"I thought that was you sneezing again," the other one said, taking his rifle off his shoulder and exhaling nervously though his Fu Manchu moustache.

"Look," Handlebar said, pointing at the sky.

And there – silhouetted against the large, yellow moon – they saw something flapping as it flew away, eventually disappearing into the darkness on the other side of the Brussels Road, the side where the English had set up their camp for the night.

"What was that?" Handlebar asked.

"If I didn't know better, I would have thought it was a flailing guy in a nightshirt," said Fu Manchu. "But then again it is only 1815, so people can't fly yet."

"True, true. But maybe we'd better go and see if everything's all right with the Generator."

They pulled up the tent flap and stepped in. The first thing they saw was that the moon was shining through a hole in the roof of the tent and that tiny, expensive-looking bits of duvet down were wafting around in the moonlight.

"What the—" Handlebar began, raising his long rifle with the almost equally long bayonet and running over to the bed, where he cried, "The Generator isn't here!"

"His duvet is missing, too!" Fu Manchu cried once he got there.

"Hi there," Nilly said, stepping into the moonlight.

The two guards jumped to attention again with their rifles at their sides.

"Pardon me, Sire. We didn't see you there, Generator, Sire!" shouted Handlebar.

"As you were, soldier," Nilly said. "That bang you just heard, do you know what that was?"

"No idea, Generator, Sire!" shouted Fu Manchu.

"That was the English trying to assassinate me. A bomb in my bed. Lucky for France I'm a type-A personality . . ."

"A what-the-huh?"

"I get up early. I was just standing here brushing my teeth."

"What?" Fu Manchu said. "But everyone knows that the French never brush their—"

"Shut up, Jacques," Handlebar said, staring into the shadows with his rifle ready. "Where did the Englishmen go and how did they get in here?"

"There was only one of them," Nilly said. "And it's actually an English woman. She's hiding in that bath."

Both of the guards spun round and aimed their rifles at the bath, which appeared to be empty.

"I didn't think the French bathed either," Fu Manchu mumbled from behind his moustache.

"Quiet, Jacques," whispered Handlebar. "You heard him. She's English."

"Shh!" Nilly ordered. "Prepare to arrest her!"

The three of them stood, very ready, staring into the bath.

"What are we waiting for?" Handlebar finally asked.

"For her to run out of air and have to come to the surface," Nilly said.

"Couldn't we just pull her up?" Fu Manchu asked.

"Well, we could try," Nilly said. "But we're talking about the great English spy Double O Point Zero Raspa Hari, who has punctured twenty-six French foil fencers in very honest duels, strangled a boa constrictor and bench-pressed four Russians. But, be my guest, go ahead."

"Nah," Handlebar said. "We're not in any hurry, are we, Jacques?"

"Nothing that can't wait," Fu Manchu said.

So all three of them continued to stand, very ready, staring into the bath.

"This lady's got herself some lungs," Fu Manchu whispered.

"Like two weather balloons," said Nilly, who'd noticed that the moonlight was fading and that the darkness was starting to take on a dawnlike grey tinge.

Just then the surface of the water opened up and there she stood: tall and thin in a black overcoat, with her two eyes wide-open over that gaping mouth revealing those small, spiky, predatory fish teeth.

"Whoa," Fu Manchu said, jumping back in fear.

"Don't move, you hideous water witch!" snarled Handlebar. "I'll shoot if you so much as twitch a nose hair!"

Raspa opened her mouth. Then closed it, opened it, closed it and so on. But she didn't move.

"Slap the handcuffs on her," Nilly yelled.

"The hand-whats?" asked Handlebar, still staring and looking quite nervous.

"No, that's right, surely those haven't been invented yet," Nilly said, scratching his scalp under that strange hat. "Rope, then. Get English spy Double O Point Zero Raspa Hari tied up. Now! That's a . . . uh, an order!"

At that, the two guards lifted the kicking, screaming, protesting Raspa out of the bath and tied her up until she looked like a corn on the cob.

"What a banshee," Handlebar said. Then he pulled off his tattered left boot, pulled off a holey left sock and stuffed it into her mouth. All of a sudden it was quiet.

"What now, Generator?"

"Frisk her!"

Handlebar did as Nilly said.

"A jar of powder," he said. "Hm, smells like strawberries."

"Toss it here," Nilly said, catching the jar that came

hurtling through the air. "And roll the spy to a dungeon. We've invented dungeons, right?"

"Um, well, yeah," Fu Manchu said, pulling Raspa onto her feet – well, onto her roller skate – and wheeling her out of the tent. "Come, beautiful spy maiden."

"You'd better go along and guard her," Nilly told Handlebar, who hadn't budged.

"But, Generator, our orders from Marshal Grouchy are to guard you at all times."

"Oh?" Nilly said. "Well, then I'm superseding that order right now. After all, I'm the one who's the . . . uh, Generator, right?"

"Of course, Generator, Sire!" Handlebar came to attention, saluted, did an about-face and marched out of the tent.

By the time the tent flap had fallen back into place behind him, Nilly had already rushed over to the bath and poured some powder from the soap jar into it. He pulled the sabre out of his belt, stuck it into the water and started stirring it around. And soon a layer of bubbles starting forming again. Nilly grabbed the jar of soap and climbed up onto the edge of the bath. He wanted to do another cannonball and lie there on the bottom wishing he were back in the Hôtel Frainche-Fraille where all the others would surely just be hanging out waiting for him by now: Lisa, Doctor Proctor and Juliette Margarine. Claude Cliché would be history and would never have met any of them. Nilly bent his knees, about to jump in.

"Puis-je entrer?" demanded a stern voice.

Nilly looked up. A man in a uniform almost as nice as his own was standing in the doorway to the tent. He was thin, tall, and had a scar that formed a *V* on one cheek.

"Good morning, Generator Napoléon."

"I don't think it's quite morning yet," Nilly said, hurriedly stuffing the jar of soap into the inside pocket of his uniform jacket.

The man just strolled right into the tent. "It looks like a little sleep has done you good, Generator. You look younger than you did yesterday."

"Oh, thank you so much," Nilly said, trying to figure out the fastest way to get this guy to leave again. "I suppose it's just the clothes. They're new, of course."

"So it's the emperor's new clothes?" the man asked, smiling, and flopped down into a chair.

"Am I the emperor?" Nilly gasped, shocked.

The man laughed. "It's up to you. But your last order was that you wanted to be addressed as Generator."

"That's what I'd surmised. Um, why did I want that again?"

"Did you forget? It's a combination of general and dictator. That makes Generator, right? Well, all right, strictly speaking it was my idea. As most things are these days." He sighed, contemplating his white gloves. "Shall we get to work then?"

"Work?" Nilly asked. "As you can see, I'm still

getting ready. I haven't even had a chance to eat my breakfast. So if you could give me a few minutes alone, Mr . . . Mr . . . ?"

The man raised his eyebrows: "It's me, Marshal Grouchy."

"Yes, of course," Nilly said, laughing nervously and sounding a tad shrill. "That's right, Emmanuel de Grouchy. Pardon me, I have so many marshals."

"You have two," Grouchy said caustically. "The other one died on the Englishmen's bayonets yesterday. You don't seem quite yourself, Generator."

"Oh, uh, yeah. I'm fine, really," Nilly said. "It's just . . . just . . . this . . . uh, nose clip."

Grouchy stood up. "If you're done washing your sabre, Sire, we have a battle to fight, Generator."

"A battle?" Nilly asked, confused. "Which battle?

"The British army is waiting on the other side of the road, Generator. Aren't you anxious to get going?"

"Very anxious," Nilly said with a gulp.

"Well, let's get going then. We're ready."

"Exactly who do you mean by 'we'?" Nilly asked, wondering if he shouldn't just jump into the bath. This guy sure wasn't backing down.

"You, me, your horse and . . ." he pulled the tent flap to the side, ". . . about seventy thousand men."

Nilly stared, his mouth hanging open. Sure enough, in the early dawn light outside the tent, he saw a magnificent white horse all saddled up. But that's not what made Nilly's mouth hang open. Behind the horse, as far as the eye could see, soldiers in blue uniform jackets with rifles and bayonets were lined up to attention.

Marshal Grouchy stepped through the tent opening.

"Greet your Generator, men!" he shouted.

The response was the synchronised roar of seventy thousand men that reverberated out over the plain: *"Vive Napoléon! Vive la France!"*

Nilly looked down at the soap bubbles just below him. He could still make it.

"Are you ready to die for your Generator, men?" Grouchy shouted.

"*Oui!*" the soldiers yelled.

Nilly was just bending his knees in preparation for the jump when a thought popped into one half of his brain. Something Juliette had said, that you only get one chance to change history. *So what?* the other half of his brain said. *Get out of here while you can!* Nilly got ready to dive into the bath. That is, he was certain that he had curled up in preparation for his cannonball, but when he looked down, he was still standing on the edge. He couldn't do it. He just simply couldn't do it. So he sighed, hopped down from the edge of the bath, stuck his sabre back into its scabbard and emerged from the tent.

A soldier was waiting and whisked him up into his saddle on the white horse. Unfortunately, during this manoeuvre the sabre ended up between Nilly's legs when he came down and it hurt so much he had to take

calm, deep breaths several times to keep from screaming out loud. Once he had managed to blink the tears
of pain out of his eyes, he noticed the army of seventy
thousand soldiers staring at him. That makes a hundred and forty thousand eyes. Minus the ones that had
lost one or both eyes in battles in Russia or Prussia, of
course. But all the two-eyed, one-eyed and zero-eyed
soldiers had one thing in common. They were all looking very stiff and rigid, with their stomachs sucked in
and their shoulders sort of back.

"At ease," Nilly yelled.

Seventy thousand men all exhaled at the same time,
relaxed their shoulders and leaned on their rifles.

Hm, Nilly thought. *Fascinating. I wonder what would
happen if I . . .*

"Smile!" Nilly yelled.

Seventy thousand slightly confused smiles appeared
before him.

"Jump!" Nilly yelled.

Seventy thousand men jumped; the ground shook when they landed.

From where Nilly sat, his hand still holding the jar of time soap bath bomb inside his jacket, he had to admit that this felt pretty cool. Yes, he felt like he could easily get used to being in charge of seventy thousand men this way. Especially if he could have some breakfast first.

A horse came up alongside him, carrying Marshal Grouchy.

"Your hat, Sire . . ." the marshal whispered out of the corner of his mouth.

"Yes?" Nilly said.

"It's on backwards."

"Backwards?"

"The point is supposed to go in the front, Generator. It looks a little . . . well, silly this way."

"Pshaw," Nilly said. "If I can decide that I should be addressed as emperor and make seventy thousand men jump, I think I ought to be able to decide which way I wear my hat. Don't you, Grouchy?"

The skin on Marshal Emmanuel de Grouchy's face went pale and looked as if it were being stretched.

"Don't you?" Nilly repeated, louder.

"Uh, yes, Generator, Sire," Grouchy said with a bow, but Nilly could see the man's jaw muscles clenching with rage. "Perhaps you should give the troops a little inspiration before the battle."

"I will," Nilly said, and turned towards his army. He took a deep breath and let his voice reverberate through the quiet morning: "My dear courageous and loyal men!"

"*Oui!*" the soldiers cheered.

"We have been fighting for a long time!" Nilly yelled.

"*Oui!*" the soldiers cheered.

"Way too long, some may think."

"*Oui!*" the soldiers cheered, but some of them gave each other questioning looks.

"Many of us haven't even had breakfast!" Nilly yelled.

The men said, *"Oui"* but less enthusiastically this time and a soft murmur was sweeping through the throng of soldiers. Out of the corner of his eye Nilly saw Marshal Grouchy's horse move closer.

"And what have we actually been fighting and dying for?" Nilly yelled. "Well, for me, a rather puny Generator, so that I could have a little more land to rule over!"

A few men shouted, *"Oui!"* while the others watched him in silence.

"Why is it so honourable to die for an emperor and a fatherland when all the emperor and the fatherland want is for you to help them out, and never the other way around?"

Grouchy's voice hissed softly at Nilly's side: "What do you think you're doing, you fool! You're ruining everything!"

But Nilly just kept going. "Here we are in a teeny tiny country that in a few years will be called Belgium. It's not going to belong to the French or the English, but to some peaceful farmers who will govern themselves, elect a prime minister every now and then, make French fries and compete in bike races. So what's the point to all this shooting at soldiers who are fighting on behalf of other stupid kings who think it's fun to amass as much land as possible, but don't really care if their subjects are happy or have anything to eat for breakfast?"

Aside from Nilly's voice and a cricket scratching an itch on its leg, there was total silence in the fields of Waterloo.

"I have a suggestion!" Nilly yelled. "And that's that we all go home now and eat breakfast!"

"*Oui!*" one single soldier shouted somewhere in the middle of the plain.

"You're crazy!" Grouchy hissed, pulling the reins tight as his horse reared. "I'm relieving you of your command, Generator!"

"I suggest," Nilly yelled at the confused soldiers. "I mean, I'm not giving this as an order, but I suggest the following. Put down your rifles, march home, give your wives and children a good hug and don't smoke in bed!"

"Oui!" a few more men shouted.

"Exercise!" Nilly bellowed. "Vote in free elections and wear your seat belts!"

"Oui!" even more men shouted.

"And don't be afraid that the people back home will call us cowards," Nilly yelled. "Marshal Grouchy here has promised me that he will tell the royal court in Paris that we fought like the idiots we are, but had to concede to superior forces!"

Grouchy's horse was rearing so wildly that the frightened marshal slid right off and landed on his bottom on the ground.

"So, what do you say?" Nilly bellowed. "Should we all just go HOME?"

This time the answer was so loud and in unison that the sky over Waterloo practically caved in, and the English on the other side of the road thought the French had fired off their first cannon salvo. Or their second, since they had shot that weird little man over earlier wearing just a nightshirt, a man so crazy he claimed he was Napoléon!

"OUI!" the French soldiers cheered. *"OUI!"*

"All right!" Nilly yelled. "But no one tell anyone what actually happened here in Waterloo. Agreed?"

"OUI!" the approximately seventy thousand soldiers yelled back.

"March home!" Nilly yelled and as he turned his horse round, he heard the rifles hitting the ground behind him. But in front of him he saw Marshal Emmanuel de Grouchy.

"Just what do you think you're doing?" growled the marshal, rubbing his tailbone. "Are you *cancelling* the Battle of Waterloo?"

"So what if I am?" Nilly said with a yawn. "So sue me."

"Sue you? I'll court-martial you!" Grouchy was so angry that his eyeballs were quivering.

"Fine," Nilly said, sliding down out of his saddle. "After my morning bath."

He hurried into the tent, but had just managed to get one foot up onto the edge of the bath when he felt something very sharp poke him in the back. He turned round and found himself face to face with Grouchy, who was holding a rapier. Nilly cursed because he saw that the tip of the deadly blade was pointing right between his eyes, just a few millimetres from his forehead.

"Tell me," Grouchy said. "*Are* you really Napoléon? Take that thing off your nose so I can see."

"Ten hut!" Nilly commanded. "Jump!"

But his brisk orders didn't seem to have any effect on the marshal.

"Guards!" Grouchy hollered without taking his eyes off Nilly. "Guards, get in here now!"

"Did someone call?" Handlebar and Fu Manchu entered the tent and stood behind Grouchy.

"Arrest this imposter!" the marshal screamed. "Tie him up and roast him over a low heat until he admits that he's an English spy. Then we'll hang him from the nearest tree."

"All right," Handlebar sighed. "Man, nothing but work, work, work."

"And what's the point to roasting him first?" sighed Fu Manchu. "Why not just hang him right away? We haven't had breakfast yet."

"Snap to it!" Grouchy howled.

"Yes, sir, Marshal." They sighed and started towards Nilly.

"Wait!" Nilly said. "The marshal is the one who should be bound."

"Interesting," Handlebar said, stopping in his tracks. "And what else?"

"Tickle the bottoms of his feet with bird feathers until he promises to be a little nicer. And then send him home to his mother with a note."

"Tie him up immediately!" Grouchy growled. "Otherwise I'll hang you too!"

"Oh, you will, will you?" Handlebar asked, swinging his rifle slightly so that it happened to be pointing right at the marshal.

Grouchy paled. "Listen up, my good men," he said. "I will promote you to lieutenants if you do as I say. Think about that: officers of the French army. And in addition, I will agree to *not* hang you. What do you say?"

Handlebar and Fu Manchu looked at each other. Then at the marshal. And finally at Nilly.

"What do you say, Generator? Do you have a better offer?"

"Yeah," Nilly said, scratching inside his ear with his left index finger. "Breakfast. Fresh-baked bread with strawberry jam."

"Fresh-baked bread," Handlebar repeated, looking at Fu Manchu.

"Strawberry jam?" Fu Manchu repeated, looking at Handlebar.

"Listen up, my good men . . ." Grouchy said. But that was also all he had time to say, because the next instant he had a holey right sock stuffed in his mouth and, after quite a bit of tying, he too had been transformed into a corn on the cob.

"Take him out and tickle him," Nilly said, and started unbuttoning his uniform. "And it would be great if you guys could hang a DO NOT DISTURB sign on the door, because I'm going to take my morning bath now."

THE ENGLISH AND the Duke of Wellington encountered no opposition that day at Waterloo. They just marched right into the Frenchmen's deserted camp. There they found countless abandoned rifles and cannons as well as a dungeon containing a half-crazed woman with a wooden leg and a long, black trench coat, plus a tent with a sign on it that said DO NOT DISTURB in French. The English, who are a very polite people, would not normally have ignored this kind of message, but since they couldn't read French, they walked right into the tent. But all they found there was a bath where the last of the soap bubbles were just disappearing.

"This is embarrassing!" the Duke of Wellington told his officers, angrily kicking the bath. "And here I was, looking forward to being a hero with huge casualty figures on both sides. And then we win without firing so much as a single shot!"

One of Wellington's officers whispered something into his ear.

"Jolly good!" Wellington exclaimed. "I've just had an idea! Listen, when we get home, we'll tell the royal court that we fought valiantly and trounced these Frenchmen. We'll say that it was the biggest battle ever! And that strange little Frenchman in the nightshirt who fell out of the sky and thinks he's Napoléon, we'll say he *is* Napoléon!" The duke laughed loudly. "And then we'll ship him off to a remote island so he can't expose our deception should he ever regain his senses!" The duke leaned over to his officers in a conspiratorial manner and whispered, "And no one tell anyone what actually happened here in Waterloo. Agreed?"

All of the officers answered in unison, "Agreed!"

NILLY WAS SITTING on a chair next to the bath in the Hôtel Frainche-Fraille. He was wearing a pair of trousers that were far too big and a shirt that he'd borrowed from Madame Trottoir at the reception desk. But at least these clothes were dry, unlike the sopping wet blue uniform he'd arrived in, which was now hanging over the back of the chair dripping. Nilly rested his head on his hands and stared sorrowfully down into the dark water. The others weren't here! He was totally alone. Apart from a seven-legged Peruvian sucking spider named Perry who was sitting inside a toothbrush glass next to a tube of Doctor Proctor's

Fast Acting Superglue on the shelf under the mirror. Perry listened quietly and seemingly sympathetically, while Nilly went on and on in despair:

"What do I do now? I can't take this anymore. You know what I want to do? Go back to when we moved to Cannon Avenue and make sure I never meet Lisa or Doctor Proctor! I can make different friends who would be way less trouble!"

Nilly reflected on this.

"All right, maybe I wouldn't have made any other friends. But I would have rather been alone than . . . well, alone, like I am now. I'm sorry to say this, Perry, but you actually aren't much company."

Nilly kicked the side of the bath so it made a deep rumbling, submarine-like sound.

Then he hopped down off the chair, left the bathroom and crawled into his bed.

The last thought he had before he fell asleep was that at least tomorrow he would get to have breakfast.

Nilly was in the middle of a dream about a sunny-side-up egg the size of a manhole cover and slices of bacon so fresh that they were still oinking when he suddenly woke up.

He'd heard something.

Something from the bathroom.

Bubbles . . . as if something were coming up from the depths . . . the depths of water, space and time . . . as if something had arrived . . . in the time-travelling bath? Nilly sat up in bed and stared through the darkness at the bathroom door, listening with his heart pounding. But there weren't any other noises.

He called out cautiously, "Lisa?"

His voice sounded so naked and lonely in the dark. Especially since there was no response from the bathroom.

"Doctor Proctor?"

Still no response.

"Juliette?"

Still nothing.

Nilly curled up under the covers. He had no desire to call out the fourth name, didn't even want to think it. Because even his thoughts stuttered at the thought of R-R-Raspa.

He lay like that for a few minutes. Nothing happened. And for guys like Nilly there's only one thing worse than when really scary things happen and that's when nothing happens. So he jumped out of bed, crept still half-undressed over to the chair where the wet uniform was hanging, pulled the sabre from the belt, tiptoed over to the bathroom door and yanked it open while screaming:

"Banzai, Englisher Schweinhund!"

Nilly stormed in swinging his sabre and slicing the darkness into three, four, yes, maybe even five pieces. It wasn't until he was sure that the darkness and everything in it had been thoroughly carved up that he flipped on the light switch. From the toothbrush glass on the shelf under the mirror, Perry stared at him in terror with his black compound eyes. But otherwise there was nothing there, at least nothing that hadn't been there before he'd gone to bed.

Wrong.

An empty wine bottle with a cork was floating in the motionless water in the bath.

He looked at it more closely. Wrong again: it wasn't empty at all.

Nilly fished the bottle out, sank his teeth into the cork and pulled until it went *plop*. Then he turned the bottle upside down and shook it. A slip of paper fell out onto the bathroom floor.

He unfolded and read it. His eyes skipped down to the bottom. The smile on his face kept growing.

It was from Lisa.

"Well, well, Perry, my old friend," he said, folding up the letter and checking his parting in the mirror. "We're in business again. Sorry to deprive you of my company, but new adventures call. Tell me, what do you know about the French Revolution and beheadings?"

Gustave Eiffel

A MAN WITH an enormous handlebar moustache, an even more enormous potbelly and a pipe between his lips was staring at the girl who had so unexpectedly appeared in his office. Not to mention the bath in which she had arrived. He squeezed his eye around his monocle, emitted a surprised "pff!" from his lips, and a cloud of tobacco smoke rose into the air between the bookshelves.

Lisa looked around. The walls were hung with drawings of buildings, bridges, breweries and other enormous things that start with *B* that you couldn't fit in a normal piece of luggage. There were two drawings on the desk under the window, two empty bottles of red wine and a pouch of tobacco. The window faced a large, open and rather empty public square. Strikingly empty, actually. Apart from all the people with parasols and top hats strolling across it. There was something strangely familiar about this square, Lisa thought.

"Who are you?" the man asked. "And where did you come from?"

"I'm Lisa," Lisa said, wringing out the sleeve of her sweater. "I come from Cannon Avenue in Norway. From sometime in the next millennium. You must be Gustave Eiffel?"

The man nodded and then had a coughing fit.

"I understand that you're afraid, Mr Eiffel," Lisa said as she climbed out of the bath.

The man waved this away dismissively, coughing, and then in a voice that was scarcely a hiss whispered, "Not at all."

His face was now as red as a peony and he was clearly struggling to get air. When he finally did manage to breathe, his throat squeaked and his lungs gurgled. Then he stuck the pipe back into his mouth, inhaled, and said with a satisfied smile:

"Nothing serious, just a touch of asthma."

It occurred to Lisa that Mr Eiffel didn't seem quite as afraid as you would expect given that an unexpected bath and a girl who said she came from the future had just appeared in his office. And a second later, she knew why.

"The professor said there would be two of you," Mr Eiffel said. "A certain Mr Nilly appears to be missing."

"You talked to Doctor Proctor?" Lisa exclaimed. "Where is he?"

Mr Eiffel stuck a thoughtful finger in between two buttons on his shirt and scratched his stomach. "Unfortunately I am not exactly sure, *moan amee*. We had a very brief meeting, right here in this very room. And then he left. But, like you, he came in a bath. A time-travelling bath, as he explained to me."

"And you believed him?" Lisa asked. "That he'd invented a way to travel through time?"

"Of course. I would have had a harder time believing the opposite, that no one would ever invent a way of travelling through time. I am an engineer after all, and I'm a hard and firm believer in people's ability to create things. All you need is a dose of imagination and a little logic." Eiffel smiled sadly. "Unfortunately, I myself only have the logic part of it, but not the imagination. If there's one thing you can never have enough of, it's imagination."

"Oh, I know a little boy who's pushing the limit," Lisa said, wringing out her wet hair over the bath.

"Really? If only I could be him right now."

"Why?"

Eiffel coughed and nodded towards the window. "Next year is the World's Fair and the Paris city council has asked me to design a tower to go in that square you see out there. They have only three requirements: that it should be beautiful, ingenious and should take the breath away from everyone who sees it. Fine . . ." Eiffel let his monocle fall into his hand, closed his eyes and rubbed his pipe against his forehead. "The problem is that I just don't have the imagination to come up with something that beautiful and ingenious. And the only thing taking away my breath is this tobacco, which isn't anywhere near strong enough. Construction has to start in a few months, and now everyone's just waiting for me to complete the design. But I can't do it. They're going to fire me and assign me to design bike racks!"

He had another coughing fit, and the red colouring climbed up his face as if he were a thermometer.

"Hogwash," Lisa said. "Of course you can draw something beautiful and ingenious."

"Afraid not," Eiffel said, choking up a little. "All I can design are broad, solid and rather ugly bridges. Like this bridge your professor came to ask me about . . ."

"Yes?"

"There's a bridge in Provence that I've already finished the drawings for. I was going to turn them in next week. He wanted me to adjust the plans, make the bridge a tiny little bit narrower. Something about hippopotamuses and their limousines . . ."

"Yes, yes!" Lisa cried. "Narrower so that Doctor Proctor and Juliette can get away and go to Rome and get married!"

"Yes, that's what he said. A touching story, I must admit it choked me up a little. And I really wasn't at all opposed to making that hideous monstrosity a little narrower. So I said yes."

"Yippee!" Lisa exclaimed jumping up and down. "Then it'll work! Then everything will be fine! Thank you so, so much, Mr Eiffel! Goodbye!" She jumped back into the bath.

"Wait a sec . . ." Eiffel said.

"I have to hurry to get back to my own time while there are still soap bubbles. I'm sure they're all waiting for me."

"Your professor didn't go back. He wouldn't let me change the plans for the bridge."

"What?" Lisa gasped, her eyes wide. "Why not?"

"We shared a bottle of wine while he told me a little about what was going to happen in the future. And then he suddenly thought of something he'd forgotten. That if the bridge were narrower, the American tanks that liberated France from Hitler in World War Two wouldn't be able to cross it. And that would be a catastrophe worse than he and Juliette not ending up together. Yes, this Hitler is going to be born very soon and as I understand it he's going to be a horrible person. So we don't want him to hold on to France."

"No, obviously not," Lisa said. "But . . . but then, well, but then everything is lost. Then Claude Cliché is going to win after all."

"Yes, that's what your Doctor Proctor said too," Eiffel said, slowly nodding his head. "So we opened another bottle of wine, drank more and both got a little upset."

"And then?" Lisa asked.

"Then I did the only thing I'm any good at," Eiffel said. "I thought about things logically."

"What do you mean?"

"Your professor told me that when Juliette's great-great-great-great-grandfather, the Count of Monte Crisco, was beheaded in the French Revolution, the family fortune was inherited by Leaufat Margarine, who had a gambling addiction. He promptly gambled it all away playing Uno. But, if the Count hadn't been

• 265 •

beheaded, he almost certainly would have had children. And then *they* would have inherited the fortune instead of this drunken lout Leaufat. And then the Margarine family would still have this fortune. And then Juliette's father wouldn't have needed to say yes to Claude Cliché's offer to save them from ruin by marrying his daughter. So I asked the professor why he didn't just go back to the Revolution and save the Count from the guillotine. Quite logical, don't you think?"

"Quite," Lisa said. "But what's a . . . uh, guillotine?"

"Oh, that," Eiffel said eagerly. "A very clever invention that the revolutionaries used to chop the heads off of counts and barons. Well, countesses and baronesses too, for that matter. Quick and efficient, chop, chop! I have the drawings for the invention around here somewhere . . ." Eiffel pulled open one of his desk drawers.

"Oh, that's really not necessary," Lisa said quickly. "So that's where Doctor Proctor went? To the French Revolution?"

"Yes, but he had to find this Count in the middle of all the chaos that was raging in Paris in 1793. So I'm not really sure exactly where he is now. Or then. Or back then. Ugh, this time-travel business is a little confusing, don't you think?" Eiffel succumbed to another coughing fit and his eyes bulged so much it looked like they were going to pop out of his head.

Lisa looked at the soap bubbles, which were already fading away in the bath. She had to hurry if she was going to make it out of here.

"So he didn't leave any kind of message behind that might make it easier for me to find him?" she asked.

"I'm afraid not," Eiffel said, shaking his head sadly. "Well, after your professor thought about it a bit, he asked me if I had a postcard and a stamp with a picture of Felix Faure from 1888. Which of course I had, since it's 1888 now and Felix Faure is the current president, right?" Eiffel laughed. "Your professor claimed that the stamp was going to be very rare and valuable someday, which is obviously completely ridiculous. Because this stamp is completely commonplace – you can find it in any house in France! But anyway I gave him the stamp and a postcard with a picture of the square you see out of the window there."

"I knew there was something familiar about that square!" Lisa exclaimed. She thought about the picture on the postcard, how she'd thought the empty public square seemed like it was missing something. And suddenly she thought she knew what it was missing . . .

"He wrote some stuff in code on the card and said it was to two friends in Oslo," Eiffel said. "A Mister Nilly and Miss Lisa. He said he was going to tell you to come to the same place he was about to go to."

"Which was . . . the, uh, French Revolution in 1793?"

"Yes, didn't you know that? He said he wrote that on the card."

"That must've been the part that got washed away. Any idea where in the French Revolution I should start looking for him?"

"Well . . ." Eiffel twisted his moustache. "I would try the Place de la Révolution, which was in front of the dreaded Bastille prison in Paris. That's where the guillotine was put to most industrious use; surely that's where the Count of Monte Crisco must have been beheaded as well."

"Thanks," Lisa said. "I'll focus on 1793, the Count of Monte Crisco and the Pastille in Paris. But there's one other thing, how did Doctor Proctor send his postcard from here?"

Eiffel chuckled at the memory. "He held the card underwater in the bath and stuck his head underwater at the same time. He said he just thought about where the card should go and – voilà! – there it went. I guess only things that are completely submerged in the water can be sent, so he stayed here."

"Interesting," Lisa said, and pointed at the empty wine bottles on the desk. "Could I borrow one of these and a piece of paper and a pencil?"

Gustave Eiffel made a sweeping gesture with his hand and said, "Help yourself."

Lisa went over to the desk, grabbed a pencil and started scribbling something on a piece of paper. Then she folded it up, stuffed it into one of the wine bottles, found two corks in the rubbish bin and shoved one into the mouth of the bottle.

"What's that?" Eiffel asked.

"A note saying where I'm going," Lisa said. "If Doctor Proctor can send things by bath post, I should be able to too."

"Sounds logical. Who's it to?"

"Nilly or Juliette. I don't know where they are, but I'm sending the note to the bath in our room at the Hôtel Frainche-Fraille."

Eiffel wasn't able to follow the last bit, because

Lisa had already stuck her head under the water along with the bottle and her words were floating up to the surface of the water like small bubbles of speech.

"There!" she said as she pulled her head back up again. "It's sent!"

"I have to hurry up and go now," Lisa said, climbing into the bath.

"I have to hurry too," Eiffel said dejectedly. "But it was very nice to meet you, Lisa. If you find the professor, give him my regards. And please don't mess history up too much."

Lisa gave him a wave and dived down.

After she was gone, Eiffel leaned over his drawings again and muttered, "*Merde*, why couldn't they just ask me to draw one of my standard ugly old bridges?" Then he noticed the sound of something dripping on the wood floor next to him and looked up. There was Lisa with her hair full of soap bubbles.

"Oh, you didn't leave after all, *moan amee*?" he asked.

"I just thought I would make a suggestion first, to thank you for all your help," she said, grabbing one of his pencils and starting to draw.

Eiffel stared wide-eyed at how her hand flew up and down, as if she knew exactly what the thing she was drawing looked like. The arches, the latticework, the four legs sloping gently outwards, almost like the legs of a bath. It was beautiful, it was ingenious, it . . . it took his breath away.

"There, like that," Lisa said. "Do you like it?"

Eiffel was overwhelmed. "Wha-what is it?"

"A tower."

"I can see that. But it's not just a tower, it's a *marvellous* tower. It's perfect! But what should I call it? The Lisa Tower?"

Lisa considered it for a second. "I think the Eiffel Tower sounds better."

"The Eiffel Tower?" The engineer had a coughing attack from sheer excitement. "You mean it? Thank you!"

"No need to thank me. Good luck!" Lisa said, and then she marched back to the bath, climbed in, mumbled "the Pastille in Paris" to herself, dived under and — voilà! — just like that she was gone.

When she surfaced again, the first thing that struck her was the stench. The second thing that struck her was the hysterical squealing and snorting. And if Lisa had been Nilly, the third thing that would have struck her would have been the thought of: *breakfast! Fresh bacon!*

But instead the third thing that struck Lisa was the end of a wooden plank that hit the back of her head. The other end was being held by an enraged farmer with a red-striped hat.

"Get out of my pigpen, you ragamuffin!" he growled. "Shh! Piggy, piggy, shh!"

The French Revolution

LISA DUCKED AS the plank came whooshing past her a second time.

She climbed out of the bathwater at once and scrambled up onto the edge of the bath.

Around and below her was a living carpet of pink

pig backs all bumping into the time-travelling bath and each other.

"Shh! Piggy, piggy, shh!" the furious farmer urged, closing in on Lisa with his plank.

Lisa jumped. She landed on one of the pig's backs, and a piercing squeal was heard above the steady drone of munching and snorting. Instinctively, she grabbed the pig's ears as it started to run. It pushed its way through the herd of pigs and continued towards the fence enclosing the pigpen, kicking up a splash of manure as it ran. When it reached the fence it lurched to a sudden stop, heaving up onto its front feet and bucking its rear end, sending Lisa sailing through the air all of a sudden. She flew over the fence, over a pitchfork, over a piglet that had strayed from the pen, and closed her eyes as she prepared for a hard landing.

Astonished when that didn't happen, she opened her eyes again and realised that she was lying on a big, soft bale of hay. Lisa stood up, brushed the hay off her clothes, and watched the farmer, who was approaching her at full speed.

Lisa was tired. Tired of being chased, tired of being afraid, tired of travelling and not finding what she was looking for, tired of not being home with her mother and father and tired of not having her teddy bear. She'd had enough. So she jumped down, pushed the piglet out of her way with her foot, grabbed the pitchfork and aimed it at the farmer.

"I'm going to skewer you and feed you to these pigs, you miserable bumpkin!" she screamed, her voice trembling with rage.

The farmer stopped suddenly and let go of the plank.

"Wha-wha-what do you want?" he asked in a gentle voice.

"I want my teddy bear!" Lisa howled, moving towards the farmer. "Apart from that, I want you to tell me the way to the Pastille! Right now! Let's hear it!"

"The P-P-Pastille?" the terrified farmer stuttered,

scrambling to get out of pitchfork range. "Well, that's . . . that's here."

"There's no prison here! Where's the Place de la Révolution?"

"Oh . . . I think you must mean the Bastille with a *B*."

Lisa's eyes lost a little of their fury. "The Bastille?"

"Yeah. That's in the middle of the city, right in front of the Place de la Révolution."

"How far away is that?"

"It's kind of a long walk, but may – may – maybe you're not in a hurry?"

"I need to get there before they behead the Count of Monte Crisco, thank you very much."

"Uh-oh," the farmer said. "Then – then you don't have much time."

Lisa lowered the pitchfork. "Why not?"

"Because they're planning to behead that Monte Crisco guy today."

Lisa tossed the pitchfork aside. "Quick! Do you have a horse I can borrow?"

"A horse?" the farmer scoffed. "I'm a pig farmer, not some yeehaw pony-pusher."

Lisa sighed. She looked around. A hairy, black pig — monstrous, the size of a motorcycle, with sharp tusks — had just rolled over in the manure, stood up and was now grunting at her menacingly. Lisa sighed again. This wasn't going to be pretty. This wasn't going to be without risk. This was going to be pig riding.

ON THIS DAY, a boy named Marcel had come to the Place de la Révolution with his parents to enjoy the crowds. "And to make sure the executioners do their jobs," his father had said.

His mother had fixed a nice packed lunch, and Marcel was looking forward to the brie and French bread. Of course Marcel didn't call it French bread, just like Spaniards don't call theirs Spanish bread, the

Danes don't say Danish bread, the Americans . . . well, you get the idea.

He just called it bread.

And brie.

And maybe a little red wine mixed with water.

They were sitting on a blanket his mother had spread out over the cobblestones in the overcrowded square. Marcel was eyeing the lunch basket longingly while his parents and the other people kept their eyes on the wooden platform up ahead of them. The executioner – a guy with no shirt on, a sweaty torso, and a black hood pulled over his head with just holes for his eyes – would read the person's death sentence in an authoritative, gravelly vibrato voice. Then he'd pull a cord and, with a whistling sound, the razor-sharp knife would plunge down from the top of the three-metre-high stand and make a *chop!* sound as it cut off the head of the poor guy who was lying below with his neck in the guillotine. The *chop* would then be followed by a cheer from the crowd.

"You see that?" The father nodded appreciatively. "That's what I call a great beheading. Did you see that, Marcel?"

But Marcel hadn't seen it. He was bored. These beheadings had been going on all summer. They'd been chopping and chopping. The heads would dance their way into the woven baskets in front of the guillotine and the blood would pour off the stage onto the cobblestones below. And every now and then, when someone had done something extra awful or had been just a little too rich or aristocratic, they would sew the head back onto the body and behead the person one more time.

No, Marcel had liked Sundays before the revolution better. Back then, he and his mother and father used to come to the Place de la Révolution and listen to musicians playing on the stage out in front of the Bastille. Marcel loved music and wanted to be a musician when he grew up. He brought the trumpet he'd been given by his grandfather with him everywhere he went.

Today was no exception. So while all the other people were absorbed in what was going on up on the stage, Marcel raised his trumpet to his lips to play a little song he'd come up with all on his own. But he never started playing because he got distracted, staring at something that was galloping down one of the side streets towards them. It wasn't pretty, it wasn't without risk. No, in fact it actually looked an awful lot like pig riding. And there was a girl sitting on the back of the monstrous black pig!

The pig stopped and the girl hopped off and ran into the crowd shouting, "Doctor Proctor! Doctor Proctor! It's me, Lisa! Are you here? Doctor Proctor!"

But the girl's voice was drowned out by the whistling of the blade, the chopping and the cheering of the crowd. The girl stopped and stood there, shouting and shouting, but got no response. Of course not, there was no way anyone could hear her delicate girl's voice. She gave up, and Marcel could see the tears welling up in her eyes as she stood there scanning the crowd in despair. Since Marcel was a sensitive boy who was more interested in music and the happiness of his fellow man than beheadings, he took his trumpet and went over to the girl.

"Hi," he said.

But the girl was too busy scanning the crowd to notice him.

Marcel cleared his throat. "Hi, Litha."

She turned and looked at him in surprise. "Did you say Lisa?" she asked.

"Yeth, Litha. That'th what I thaid. Do you need thome help?" Marcel asked.

"How did you know my name?" the girl asked.

"Becauthe you hollered 'It'th me, Litha' theveral timeth."

"Oh, right," Lisa said, smiling, but it wasn't a happy smile, more like an about-to-cry smile.

"Your voithe doethn't carry that well becauthe of

all the noithe from all theeth people," Marcel said. "If you want thith Doctor Proctor fellow to hear you, you need thomething loud. Thith, for exthample." Marcel held out his trumpet. "And maybe you ought to take that thtrange clip off your nothe."

Lisa looked at his instrument. "I can't shout his name with that."

"No," Marcel said. "But maybe I could play thome-thing that would make him underthtand that you're here."

"What would that be?"

"I don't know. Ithn't there a Doctor Proctor thong? Or a Litha thong?"

Lisa looked discouraged and shook her head.

Marcel cocked his head to the side. "Maybe a thong from the plathe you're from?"

"A Cannon Avenue thong, I mean, song?" Lisa said. "I don't think so."

"Well, then," Marcel sighed, thinking for a minute.

"Would you like a thlitce of bread with thome brie and pâté?"

Lisa stared at Marcel's trumpet. Imagining is imagining, she thought. And dreaming is just dreaming. Or maybe not.

"Could I borrow your trumpet?" she asked.

Marcel looked first at her and then down at his instrument. He hesitated. But then he nodded and handed her the trumpet. She put her lips to the mouthpiece, concentrated to block out the sound of yet another *swish!* — *chop!* — *hurrah!* Because this was what she had dreamed of. Not that it would happen in a place where people's heads were being chopped off, exactly, but still: playing this song for a large crowd.

She placed her fingers over the keys like Nilly had taught her and then she blew. The first note quivered, hesitant and timid. The second was flat and sounded awful. The third was just wrong. But the fourth was right. Marcel nodded in approval as the sixth note rose, clear and strong, into the blue afternoon sky over the Place de la Révolution in Paris. It's funny to think about this, but no one other than you and me know that this was the first time in history that anyone in France – and anyone anywhere in the world for that matter – heard a song that wouldn't be written for another sixty-something years, a song that every Norwegian would one day recognise, a song that would go on to become the Norwegian national anthem, "Ja, vi elsker".

The notes pierced through the noise of the crowd and made everyone turn around to listen. Even the executioner up on the stage, who'd been nicknamed Bloodbath because of his efficiency, stopped his work, cocked his ears under his black executioner's hood and scratched his naked barrel-shaped torso. He thought it was quite a captivating melody. All it lacked was . . . well, what was it missing, actually? An accordion maybe? Bloodbath was roused from his musical contemplations by the fact that the guy with his head currently locked into the guillotine, a thin beanpole with some weird eyeglasses that looked like they were glued onto his face, started yelling and shouting in some strange foreign language:

"Nilly! Lisa! Here! I'm up here!"

Lisa stopped playing and looked around, her heart pounding, because there was no doubt about whose voice that was. He rolled his *R*s like a rusty old lawnmower. It was Doctor Proctor! She jumped up and down, trying to see where his voice was coming from.

"Why don't you thit up on my thoulderth tho you can thee," Marcel offered.

"Are you sure you're strong enough?" Lisa asked, looking sceptically at the skinny boy.

"Of courth," Marcel said, kneeling down.

Lisa climbed onto his shoulders and Marcel stood up, staggering and wobbling.

"I'm over here!" Doctor Proctor called. "Quick! The situation is a little, uh . . . urgent!"

"Oh no . . ." Lisa said, losing hope. Up on the stage she saw a thin, bony man with scraggly, dishevelled hair over a pair of sooty motorcycle goggles, who was screaming in a language she assumed was Norwegian, as Lisa was still wearing the French nose clips. Doctor Proctor!

"What ith it?" Marcel groaned underneath her.

"Doctor Proctor is in the guillotine! They're going to behead him! We have to save him!"

Lisa swung herself off, slid down Marcel's back and started running forwards, pushing her way through the crowd.

"No!" Marcel shouted. "They behead anyone who trieth to thtop people from being beheaded! Litha!"

But Lisa wasn't listening, she was just forcing her way through.

Bloodbath's grave, vibrato voice rang out from the stage: "The Revolutionary Court of Paris has sentenced Doctor Victor Proctor to beheading because he tried to prevent the beheading of this fellow here . . ."

Bloodbath stuck his hand down into the woven basket, picked up a head by its hair and held it up to the attentive audience.

". . . the recently deceased Count of Monte Crisco!"

The crowd erupted into cheers.

Lisa had almost reached the stage, but was stuck behind a tall person who wouldn't budge. "Please let me through!" Lisa cried loudly, using the trumpet to poke the person in the shoulder.

The person slowly turned to stare at Lisa, smiled broadly and whispered, in a voice as dry as a desert wind, "Ship ahoy, there you are. Let me give you a hug!"

Lisa felt everything freeze into ice. The blood that ran in her veins, the scream she had on her lips, yes, even time seemed to stop moving as a couple of arms — thin, but as strong as steel wires — coiled around her. The breath hit her at near gale force and reeked of stinky socks.

Bloodbath tossed the Count of Monte Crisco's head back into the basket and put a pair of glasses on over his mask. He started to read aloud from a document.

"The jury had the following to say about the condemned: 'Doctor Victor Proctor is a funny guy who speaks well for himself. But he chose the wrong tactic and made a nasty mistake when he argued before the court today that he had just invented a time-travelling bath that—'"

The audience laughed in delight and Bloodbath had to wait for a moment before he could proceed.

Meanwhile Lisa squirmed in vain in the tall woman's iron grip.

"Let me go!" she roared, but the woman's arms remained locked tight.

"Calm down, child," the woman whispered into her ear. "Let's enjoy the conclusion together. After this, the invention will be all mine, don't you see?"

She had the same sharp teeth and black eye

make-up as before, but what made Raspa seem even more terrifying than she had in Lisa's imagination was that frenzied, crazed gleam in her eye.

"Now, Lisa, are you trying to save that poor slob up there?" Raspa asked, nodding towards the guillotine and Doctor Proctor, who was staring out over the crowd in desperation while Bloodbath read the rest of the sentence to occasional jeers from the audience, which was clearly starting to get bored.

"Whatever," Lisa groaned. "If they cut off his head, I could just travel back in time a few hours and save him then."

Raspa laughed and shook her head. "It's not as easy to change history as you idiots obviously think it is. Haven't you noticed that? Not even Victor seems to understand that it's impossible to change what's happened without giving up your life. Or have you forgotten what I told you in the shop? History is carved in stone and you can only change what's written if you're willing to die."

Now Lisa remembered. Was that why they hadn't managed to prevent anything from happening?

"Why do you know more about changing history than Doctor Proctor?" she asked to win herself some time as she tried to wriggle her hand that was holding the trumpet free.

"Because no one has studied or knows more about time than me, my girl. After all, I was the one who invented the time soap bath bomb."

"Time soap bath bomb?" Lisa groaned. She thought about the clocks in the Trench Coat Clock Shop and knew instinctively that Raspa was telling the truth. But she also realised something else at the same time.

"But . . . but if history is carved in stone, then Doctor Proctor can't die now! If he did, fartonaut powder would never be invented, which would change history. And that's not possible. At least according to you."

"You're not hearing what I'm saying, you stupid girl," Raspa said, letting her black made-up eyelids slide down over her enormous eyeballs and lowering her voice. "Death is the exception. Only if you die can you change history. Because then you yourself disappear into time and never come back. And, see? It's about to happen now. Victor is about to die, to disappear forever, which will change history." Her eyes were open wide, and there was an icy laughter in her voice: "It will all be mine and only mine!"

Lisa had managed to tug her arm halfway free, but couldn't get it any further.

"What do you mean *it will all be yours?*"

"If Victor Proctor dies in 1793, who do you think will patent the time-travelling bath? Who will become the greatest inventor in the world?"

Up on the stage Bloodbath stopped reading. He skimmed down the rest of the page and then shouted over the increasing chorus of boos, "All right, people, there's a bunch of other stuff here, but it's pretty much the same as all the others. So I suggest that we get on with it."

Enthusiastic cheering.

Raspa tilted her head back and laughed an absolutely gruesome laugh.

Lisa seized this opportunity to try one final, vigorous tug. She got one hand free from Raspa's grasp.

"Hey, you miserable landlubber—" Raspa began, but didn't make it any further. A trumpet hit her on the head and the towering spectacle of a woman listed to the side and then capsized.

Lisa hurried, sneaking under the arms of the guards who were stationed on either side of the stairs, and ran up the steps onto the stage. There she jumped up onto the back of Bloodbath, who was already holding the cord preparing to release the knife blade.

"Stop!" she screamed. "Doctor Proctor is innocent! You're making a mistake!"

Bloodbath twitched his back, as if what had landed on him wasn't much more than a fly. "Guards!" he yelled.

"We're coming!" a voice responded.

"Forgive us, Mr Bloodbath," another voice said.

And immediately thereafter Lisa felt strong arms ripping her off Bloodbath's back and holding on to her tightly. There were three faces in front of her:

A blotchy face with a Fu Manchu moustache.

An equally blotchy face with a handlebar moustache.

And one that wasn't a face at all but a black mask with holes for the eyes.

"You are trying to stop a beheading," growled Blood-bath, pointing a trembling finger at her. "I accuse you and demand that you be beheaded. Does the accused have anything to say?"

Lisa gasped. "I, uh . . . the professor, uh . . . we're innocent!"

"And what does the jury have to say?" Bloodbath growled, staring at Handlebar and Fu Manchu.

"I, uh . . . I . . ." stammered Handlebar. "She's just a little girl."

"Just a little girl, yes," Fu Manchu said. "So I, as far as I'm concerned, uh . . ."

Bloodbath stared at them. "Is there anyone else here who wants to try to stop a beheading?" he growled in a deep voice.

"She's guilty!" yelled Handlebar.

"Guilty!" yelled Fu Manchu.

Bloodbath walked over to the guillotine and opened the pillory holding Doctor Proctor in place.

"There's room for one more. Get her over here. Let's make it a double-header!"

The guards pushed her head down next to Proctor's. Then the pillory slammed back into place over their necks and they were locked in.

"Hi, Professor," Lisa said. "Nice to see you again." She craned her neck struggling to look sideways, but it was quite difficult since her head was locked in.

"Hi, Lisa," Doctor Proctor said. "I'm sorry I got you into this mess. Really very sorry."

"Don't worry about it. It's not that important," Lisa said, tilting her head back so she could look up and see a little of the sky over the crowd. And up above, a few metres over them, the sun gleamed on a very shiny, very sharp knife blade.

"Then give me a CHOP!" shouted Bloodbath, holding on to the cord. "Ready, everyone?"

"*OUI!*" the answer rang out from the Place de la Révolution.

"Give me a *C!*" Bloodbath cried.

"*C!*" the crowd shouted.

"Give me an *H!*"

"*H!*"

"I'm supposed to say hi to you from a bunch of people," Lisa said. "Anna from Innebrède, Gustave Eiffel and Juliette, of course."

"Oh, Juliette," Proctor whispered, tearing up and closing his eyes. "I've failed Juliette . . ."

Lisa's eyes welled up too. And maybe that's why she thought she saw what she saw, as she looked out over the crowd and caught sight of Raspa's face there in the second row. Because it really looked like Raspa had tears in her eyes too.

"Give me an *O*!"

"*O!*"

"Give me a *P*!" Bloodbath shouted.

"*P!*"

Behind her, Lisa heard Bloodbath hurriedly ask the guards in a whisper: "Is there only one *P* in 'chop' or two?"

"I'm going to go with one," Handlebar whispered.

"I think it's obviously two," Fu Manchu said.

Lisa blinked away a tear. So this was how it would end. The sun was shining, the air smelled of jasmine and freshly baked bread and she could hear birds sing-ing and pigs oinking in the distance. Her eyes filled with tears again. Was she really never going to see her mother or father or Nilly again? She blinked two more times. Something was dancing over the top of people's heads out there, maybe a butterfly.

"Give me another half a *P*!" Bloodbath shouted.

"*P!*"

A blue butterfly. With white trousers. And a three-cornered hat that was on backwards. And it was heading this way.

"What does that spell?" Bloodbath shouted.

"CHOP(P)!"

"I can't quite hear you."

"CHOP(P)!"

The butterfly was getting bigger. It was getting clearer. Lisa could tell now that it wasn't flying, but jumping from one person's head to another's, making its way over the top of the crowd. And it had . . . freckles?

"What do we do now?" roared Bloodbath.

"CHOP!"

It was . . . it couldn't be . . . but it was . . . IT WAS NILLY!

How wonderful! Oh, and how awful! Because it was too late. Lisa heard Bloodbath yank on the cord; the birds stopped singing and the pigs stopped oinking. The only thing you could hear now was the whistle of the blade on its way down.

Head over Heels

A NOTE SANG out in the air, and that note was the sound of the edge of a freshly released knife blade racing towards Lisa's and Doctor Proctor's necks. Soon it would separate their heads from their bodies and history would be changed. No girl named Lisa would ever live in the red house in Cannon Avenue and no

Doctor Proctor would ever live in the blue one. Fart powder, fartonaut powder and French nose clips would never be invented. And the time-travelling bath would be invented by someone else, specifically Proctor's rather evil assistant, Raspa. True, Nilly was on his way towards the stage, but he was too late. Bloodbath had already released the guillotine blade.

Future prospects were – in other words – rather bleak.

Lisa closed her eyes.

Then the knife was there, and the whistling stopped with a loud clang.

Lisa was dead. Of course she was dead, she'd just been decapitated and besides she was surrounded by a deathly silence. True, it was a little weird that the sound the blade had made when it hit her was *clang!* instead of *chop!* but so what? When she thought about it, it was a little weird that she had heard any sound at all since she didn't have a head anymore. Actually it was weird that she was thinking all this stuff what with being headless and all. Lisa hesitantly opened her eyes, half expecting to see the inside of a woven basket and – above her – her own headless body. Instead she was looking out at the crowd, which was staring at her and the professor, speechless, their mouths open, looks of disbelief on their faces.

Then she heard a familiar voice:

"Dear citizens of Paris! The day of liberty has arrived! Just as my sabre has saved these two innocent children of the revolution, it will liberate you, yes, YOU, from tyranny, exploitation, corrosion and other miseries!"

Lisa turned her head. Just above her own and the professor's necks, she saw a sabre blade with its tip jammed into the guillotine. The sabre had obviously stopped the guillotine blade at the last possible nanosecond before they'd both become headless. Or bodyless. Depending on how you looked at it. Next to her she heard the professor moan quietly, "Are we still alive?"

"Yup," Lisa whispered, her eyes following the blade of the sabre out to its handle, to the small hand holding on to the sabre and to the little guy in the blue uniform who was addressing the crowd while gesticulating wildly with his free hand: "I promise to lower all conceivable kinds of taxes and fees on tobacco, petrol, toys and holiday cruises!"

"Nilly!" Lisa hissed quietly. "What are you doing?"

Nilly stopped and whispered, "Shh! I'm good at this. I recently convinced seventy thousand guys with rifles to go home. Just listen . . ."

Nilly cleared his throat and raised his voice again. "I will do away with toothaches, PE lessons and that slushy, sticky snow that's no good for skiing on. And I will do away with the death penalty. Especially for nutty professors and quarrelsome girls. If you will agree with me on this, everyone will get a PlayStation for Christmas!"

He lowered his voice again and whispered, "You see? They're nodding. I'm winning them over."

"Not quite, I'm afraid," Doctor Proctor said.

And the professor appeared to be right. An irritated murmur was spreading through the crowd. A few people were shaking their fists at the stage.

"We want a beheading!" a voice screamed from somewhere in the crowd.

"We want to see this little guy's head chopped off too!" someone else yelled.

Behind him on the stage Bloodbath had recovered from the shock of seeing a little boy come swooping in, jabbing his sabre into the guillotine to stop the blade and – even worse – possibly dulling the blade so that it would have to be sharpened yet again. But this little boy was obviously a raving lunatic, so Bloodbath and the two guards approached him from behind with the greatest of care.

"But my dear countrymen." Nilly laughed

good-naturedly. "Aren't you listening? I'm going to do away with rain on Sundays!"

A slice of bread with brie on it came sailing out of the crowd and was about to strike Nilly. He turned to avoid it and caught sight of Bloodbath and the two guards, who had their swords drawn.

"And a raise for everyone!" Nilly cried, but he didn't look that confident anymore. "Especially . . . uh, executioners and guards with moustaches. What do you guys say to that?"

But no one said anything to that. Bloodbath and the guards just continued to slowly close in on him, as did the crowd, its threatening murmur getting louder and louder.

"Darn it! I don't get it," Nilly mumbled. "This worked so well at Waterloo!"

"You'd better think of something else," Doctor Proctor said. "And fast. They're going to rip us to shreds."

"Well, like what?" Nilly whispered. "I've already promised them everything! What do these people actually like?"

"I think," Lisa said, "they like . . . music."

"Music?" Nilly asked dubiously.

"Behead the little guy twice!" someone bellowed and several others said, "*Oui!*"

Nilly looked around in despair. He knew the game was almost up. Soon, but not quite yet. Because wasn't he a resourceful little guy who knew a thing or two? Maybe. He could run fast, he could lie so well that even he believed himself and he could play the trumpet so that even the birds would weep with joy, and—

The trumpet!

He looked at the brass instrument that Lisa was still holding in her hand. And the next second he let go of his sabre, hopped down from the guillotine, ducked under the guards' arms and snatched the trumpet. He put it right to his lips and blew.

The first two notes rose up towards the blue sky and just like that the larks and warblers stopped singing and the bees and blowflies stopped buzzing. As the third and fourth notes surged out of the trumpet, the threatening murmurs fell silent as well. Because unlike the Norwegian national anthem, this song was one everyone in the crowd had heard before.

"Isn't that . . . ?" said a buxom woman with two children on each arm.

"Why it has to be . . ." said a farmer, using his pitchfork to scratch himself under his warm, red-striped hat.

But Nilly didn't get any further, because then the two guards grabbed him under his arms.

"Get him into the guillotine," Bloodbath shouted. "He tried to prevent two beheadings, which means we need to behead him three times! What do you say, people? Give me a *C!*"

"*C!*" replied the crowd. True, not as loudly or

enthusiastically as Bloodbath had expected, but if there was one thing he knew it was how to whip them into a bloodthirsty mood:

"Give me a—"

"No!" The voice came from the crowd and was so small and frail that Bloodbath could have easily drowned it out. But it threw him so much that he simply forgot to continue. In his time as executioner no one at the Place de la Révolution had ever talked back to him, protested or spoken out against what had been decided. Because everyone knew that was tantamount to asking to be a head shorter themselves.

"Let him play the trumpet," cried the voice. "We want to hear muthic! The way it uthed to be here on Thundayth."

Not a sound was heard in the Place de la Révolution. Bloodbath gaped at the crowd, his face contorting into an enraged grimace, which no one could see because of his hood.

"Who said that?" he roared.

"Me," the voice said. "Marthell."

"Marthell?" Bloodbath repeated. "Marthell, now you're going to—"

"I agree with Marcel," another voice said. This one was hoarse and dry as a desert wind. "We want to hear the rest of the song. After all, it is the Marseillaise."

Bloodbath was speechless again. He was staring at a bizarre, black-haired witch of a woman in a black trench coat.

"I want to hear the song," called a voice from the very back of the crowd, followed by two approving pig grunts.

"Me too!" yelled a woman.

"And me! Play the Marseillaise, kid."

Bloodbath turned towards the two guards.

"Humph!" he said. Then he gave a dissatisfied nod and they released Nilly. Not waiting to be asked a second time, Nilly put the trumpet to his lips and started playing. He wasn't far into the first verse before people started singing along. Hesitantly at first, then more earnestly.

> *"Contre nous de la tyrannie*
> *L'étendard sanglant est levé."*

Or, for those of you who don't have your French nose clips on at the moment:

> *"The bloody banner of tyranny*
> *is raised against us."*

Nilly leaped up onto the guillotine so that he was straddling the heads of Doctor Proctor and Lisa, both of whom were singing at the tops of their lungs:

> *"To arms, citizens,*
> *form your battalions.*

Let's march, let's march!

May impure blood

fill our gutters."

There was no doubt about it. Those were some catchy lyrics. And even after Nilly stopped playing, people kept on singing. Out of the huge number of people singing, Nilly was able to pick out three voices: a high, frail voice with a bit of a lisp. A hoarse, desert-like voice. And behind him, Bloodbath's gravelly vibrato.

"Let us release everyone who's been sentenced to death," Nilly screamed when the song was over. "We don't want any more death. Because what do we want . . . ?"

"What do we want?!" the people in the Place de la Révolution cried.

"Give me an *L*!" Nilly shouted.

"*L!*"

"Give me an *I*!"

"I!"

"Give me a *F*!"

"*F!*"

Give me an *E*!"

"*E!*"

"And what does that spell?"

"Life!" the crowd answered. "Life! Life!"

By this point Nilly was so excited, worked up, ecstatic and inspired that he just had to start singing. So he did, "There will be life here – yes, yes! And not death – no, no!"

Bloodbath ran over to the guillotine, unlocked it, got Lisa and Doctor Proctor out and onto their feet again as he brushed off their clothes and asked with concern if they were all right. Obviously they were because they ran right over to the little lad in the uniform, each grabbed one of his arms and they lifted him up while he kept singing, "There will be life here – yes, yes!"

Down in front of the stage people had started dancing and jumping up and down as they sang along. People were more animated than they'd been even during the bloodiest and most successful Sunday beheadings. Bloodbath felt a strange warmth, yes, a sense of joy spreading through his body at the sight of them, a delight that surged through him. It couldn't be stopped, there was something about this irritating, simple little song. So, once the delight reached his throat, Bloodbath did something he had never done before in his entire career as Paris's most dreaded executioner. He pulled off his hood and allowed people to see his face. And then, in an instant, the crowd stopped singing. They stared at him, appalled, because Bloodbath was not at all a good-looking man. But then he smiled broadly and chimed in his booming vibrato, "There will be life here – rah, rah!"

And with that, the party was in full swing again. People ran amok. They were crazed, frenzied, zany, brazen, pizzazzy and a bunch of other things with *Z*s in them. They didn't even notice the three people sneaking away behind the stage, round the corner of the dreaded Bastille prison building, and disappearing. They just kept singing and dancing and splashing red wine on each other. The song was long forgotten by the next day when most of them woke up with throbbing heads, aching hips and sore throats, but not by Bloodbath. Bloodbath would keep singing this song for the rest of his life and would later teach it to his children and grandchildren, who would eventually move around quite a bit, to England, to Germany – and some of them even to a small town in Minnesota, where they would form the heavy metal band Meat Ball, which would become famous after being featured in the mockumentary *There Will Be Life Here*.

"DID YOU BRING the time soap bath bomb?" Proctor asked breathlessly. He and Lisa and Nilly had left the Bastille behind and were now racing through the crooked streets of Paris. Lisa and Nilly had no idea where they were, but the professor seemed to know his way through the quiet Sunday alleys and lanes.

"I have a smidge," Lisa said. "But I don't think it's enough for all three of us. I had to take a few detours to get here, you know."

"I have a smidge," Nilly said. "But I don't think it's enough for all three of us. I had to take a few detours to get here, you know."

"Let's hope if we combine it, it'll be enough," Doctor Proctor said as they came round a corner. "Have you guys seen Juliette? Is she waiting at the hotel?"

But before they were able to answer, Doctor Proctor stopped so suddenly that Lisa and Nilly ran right into him.

"Oh no!" the professor said. "Someone stole my bath. Look!"

But there wasn't much to see since what he was

pointing to was an empty square with just a few empty market stalls in it.

"Well, I guess someone got themselves a new bath," Nilly mumbled. "What are we going to do now?"

"Where's your bath, Nilly?" Lisa asked.

"Where you said you were going on that message in the bottle," Nilly said. "The Pastille. Weird destination, by the way. I wound up in the middle of a big chicken coop."

"Sorry, I mixed up Pastille and Bastille," Lisa said. "If we don't have enough soap, we'll have to get there before the bubbles are gone. But how will we get there? We don't have any pigs."

"Pigs?" the professor and Nilly cried in unison.

"Forget about it," Lisa sighed, realising that it would be too hard to explain. "What are we going to do now?"

"Yeah, what are we going to do?" the professor and Nilly cried in unison.

The three friends stared at each other.

And as they stood there staring at each other, stymied, in the sunshine filtering down between the tall Parisian buildings, they heard the lively clopping of horseshoes and the creaking of large wooden wheels. They turned round. A brown horse with large black blinkers came prancing round the corner. And behind it, a carriage. A driver was sitting on the front of the carriage, swaying back and forth and looking like he was about to fall asleep. He had big bags under his eyes, a tattered coat and a moth-eaten top hat, black and tall as a stovepipe.

"Need a lift?" he asked with a yawn.

"That's just what we need!" the professor exclaimed. "Come on!"

They climbed in the door of the carriage, which started moving right away.

There was just exactly enough room for four people on the two benches, and that was also just what they needed, because there was already one person sitting in there. The brim of the passenger's top hat had slipped down over his eyes and he was obviously sound asleep, because his body was flopping back and forth as the carriage moved.

"Weird," Lisa said.

"What is?" the professor asked.

"The driver didn't ask us where we were going."

"Elementary." Nilly smiled condescendingly. "Obviously he's going to drop this other passenger off first."

"But we don't have time for that!" Lisa said. "Should we wake him up and ask if it's okay if we go to the Pastille first?"

The professor shook his head. "I'm afraid that won't help, Lisa. I'm sure the bubbles will already be long gone."

They sat there for a while contemplating this, and the only thing that broke the silence was the sound of the horse's hooves, clopping against the cobblestones in a slow tap dance.

"Raspa was there," Lisa said. "In the crowd. Did you see her?"

"No," Doctor Proctor said. "But I'm not surprised."

"Oh?" Lisa and Nilly said, looking at the professor, shocked.

"That was the idea – for her to follow you guys to Paris," he sighed.

"The idea?" Nilly and Lisa yelled, you guessed it, in unison.

"Yeah. I sent you two down to her shop with that stamp so she would understand that I had succeeded in travelling through time, that I had got our invention to work. I knew that once she understood that, she would try to find out where I was and then come to steal the invention from me. Like she had tried to do when she was my assistant here in Paris."

"Steal the invention from you!" Lisa exclaimed, agitated. "Why would you want her to come here, if that's what she was going to do?"

"Because I was out of the time soap bath bomb," the professor said. "And because I knew there was enough in that jar in the cellar to bring you two here but not to bring all three of us back. Raspa is the only one in the world who can make more soap. I needed her here, simple as that."

"Why couldn't you just send Raspa a postcard and ask her to come?" Nilly asked.

The professor sighed again. "Raspa would never have voluntarily come to rescue me. She hates me."

"Why?"

Doctor Proctor scratched his head. "I've wondered about that a lot, but I really don't know. I never tried to deprive her of the honour of having invented the time soap bath bomb."

"But . . ." Nilly said. "How did you know that we would spill the beans so she would find out we were going to Paris?"

The professor smiled wryly. "First of all, there was

the stamp and the postcard, which I knew would make her understand the situation. Second of all, you're a whiz at a lot of things, Nilly, but keeping secrets isn't exactly your speciality, is it?"

Lisa cleared her throat.

"Eh heh heh," Nilly chuckled with a zigzag smile.

"But what do we do?" Lisa said. "How do we find Raspa and get her to make more soap?"

"Well," the professor said. "Finding her won't be that hard."

"Oh?"

"You think horse-drawn carriages just show up out of thin air right when you need them?"

Doctor Proctor nodded towards the sleeping passenger, and then looked down. Nilly and Lisa followed his gaze down to the floor. And there – jutting out from under the edge of the trench coat – was a wooden leg that ended in a roller skate.

Where Is Juliette?

THE HORSE-DRAWN CARRIAGE jostled back and forth over the streets of Paris. Lisa, Nilly and Doctor Proctor sat inside it, staring at their strange travelling companion.

"So that's it?" a hoarse voice grumbled from under the rim of the top hat. "So that's why you wanted me back, Victor? To make more time soap bath bomb for you and these brats?"

As the top hat was pushed up onto the top of the passenger's head, Raspa's searing eyes emerged to glare at Doctor Proctor.

"Yes, of course," Doctor Proctor said.

"Yes, of course!" hissed Raspa, throwing her top hat to the floor. "Because that's all I ever was to you, isn't it, Victor? A lousy soap maker!"

"Quite the contrary," the professor said, taken aback. "You were a brilliant soap maker. The best, actually."

"But a soap maker all the same. Never . . . never . . ." Raspa's voice quivered a little. "Never anything more."

"What do you mean, Raspa?"

She stared at Doctor Proctor, her chest rising and falling.

"Nothing," she said, suddenly sounding as if she had a cold. "And now, Victor, now you think she's there at the Hôtel Frainche-Fraille waiting for you, that . . .

that . . ." She waved her hand dismissively and spat out the name, "Juliette Margarine!"

Nilly looked from Raspa to Doctor Proctor. He didn't understand what was going on and it looked like the professor – who usually understood so much – was also clueless.

Only Lisa appeared to be keeping up with the situation. At any rate, she leaned over towards Raspa and asked, "Where's Juliette?"

The woman with all the black eye make-up laughed like a croaking crow. "And why should I tell you that?"

"Now you listen here, Raspa—" Doctor Proctor started threateningly, but was interrupted.

"Don't worry, Victor. Let's just say that she's getting what she deserves. Forget about that woman. She was never the one for you anyway, that witch."

"Witch . . . ? Ouch!" The professor had stood up in the carriage, smacking his head on the roof. "No one calls the woman I love a witch!"

"Victor, please," Raspa laughed. "A man of your age shouldn't be getting worked up like this. Think about your heart."

"At least I have a heart," the professor snarled. "While you . . . you . . ." Big professor tears welled up in his eyes. "You just have a big, cold brain!"

"Raspa, *where* is Juliette?" Lisa repeated. "She travelled somewhere in time, didn't she? You tracked her using the soap residue, didn't you?"

Raspa sighed deeply. "I don't know how much time soap bath bomb you have left, but if you have any I suggest you use it to get back to your own time. That's where I'm planning on going anyway." She leaned back in her seat, crossing her foot over her wooden leg.

"Raspa . . ." whispered a tearful Doctor Proctor as a humongous, gigantic professor tear rolled down his cheek. "Please! Just tell me what you want in exchange for telling me where Juliette is and I'll give it to you."

Raspa raised an eyebrow. "Anything?"

"Anything! Don't you understand? If I can't have Juliette, I might as well be dead."

Raspa shivered at his words, as if they'd stung her like peas from a slingshot.

"Oh really?" she said sharply, lifting her chin. "Well then draw out the plans for the time-travelling bath and give them to me. Ha!"

"Sure thing!" cried Doctor Proctor, smiling. "You can have the whole invention to yourself. And all the other inventions I've come up with, actually. They're all yours!"

Raspa's mouth opened, but at first nothing came out. She closed it again, opened it and tried again. "Do you mean . . ." she whispered. "Do you mean that you would give me everything just for . . . that woman?"

"Yes, I do," Doctor Proctor said quickly. "You have my word. No matter what you think of me otherwise, you know I always keep my word."

Raspa stared at him, her mouth gaping.

"Well?" the professor said.

"It's a deal," Raspa said, barely audibly. "So . . ."

She took a breath, and the only thing you could hear in the carriage was the clopping of horse feet, cows mooing in the distance and a sound that almost sounded like snoring. "When I managed to break open the door to the room you guys were staying in at the Hôtel Frainche-Fraille, the little girl and boy had already left via the bath. But Juliette was still there. I threatened her with my old, but completely functional, pistol. I ordered her into the bath, then grabbed hold of her hair, submerged my own head, concentrated, and sent her to where she is now. The same way you sent your postcard, Victor."

"Hm," the professor concurred. "And where did you send her?"

"Someplace where she couldn't run away or be found, of course. After all, she was all I had . . . how should I put this . . . to negotiate with."

Doctor Proctor gulped. "Where? Out with it."

"To a jail cell. In the city of Rouen. On May thirtieth. In the year 1431."

Doctor Proctor looked puzzled. "Why there? Why then?"

"I know," Lisa said.

"Oh?" Doctor Proctor said, and looked at her.

"Mrs Strobe just covered that in history class. Joan of Arc was burned at the stake in the Old Market Square in Rouen on that date."

"Is that true?" the professor asked, looking at Raspa.

Raspa shrugged. "It was the first thing I thought of."

"Something tells me our troubles aren't over yet," Doctor Proctor said.

Just then the carriage stopped and they heard the driver's voice call from the roof, "The Pastille, Mademoiselle Raspa!"

"So this is where you were going too?" Doctor Proctor asked.

"Of course," Raspa said. "My bath is here. In the pigsty, to be precise."

"You followed me," Lisa said.

"Yes. I realised that one over there was never going to lead me to Victor," Raspa said, nodding towards Nilly, who you're probably thinking has been quiet for quite a while now, which is pretty unlike him. Nilly was lying slumped down in the seat, and the sound that almost sounded like snoring actually was just that: snoring.

Lisa rolled her eyes and gave Nilly a kick in the shin so that he opened his eyes. He blinked, smacked his lips, smiled and mumbled a very groggy, but hopeful, "Breakfast?"

They hurried out of the carriage. Luckily the baths were still right where they'd left them. Sure, they had to pull out three pigs, who were enjoying the bathwater, and in the chicken coop the rooster was perched on the edge of the bath pecking at them aggressively. He obviously thought the bath now belonged to him.

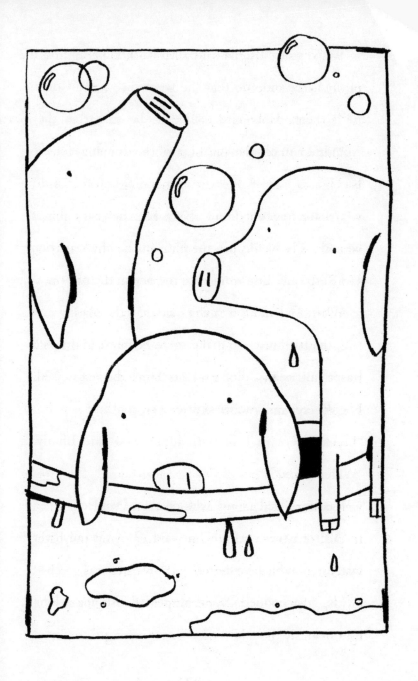

Raspa poured some time soap bath bomb into both of the baths and said that she wanted to go to Rouen with them. How else could she be sure that they wouldn't run off and cheat her of the drawings for the bath?

Doctor Proctor didn't object and they agreed that he and Nilly would use the bath in the chicken coop and Raspa and Lisa would use the one in the pigsty.

When Lisa and Raspa were alone in the pigsty, stirring the bathwater to make some bubbles, Lisa heard Raspa sniffle. Lisa didn't say anything. She just waited. Then there was another sniffle. And another.

"You were in love with him," Lisa said finally. "Weren't you?"

Raspa sniffled a long, wet, oversized sniffle.

"Victor never noticed," she said. "He was only ever interested in his inventions."

Lisa just nodded. She'd suspected this for a long time.

"I would have done anything for him," Raspa said, sniffling and still stirring. "I would have gladly given him the recipe for the stupid time soap bath bomb if he'd only just asked. I thought he was a little slow, that he just needed a little time to fall in love with me. But I realised that he wasn't slow at all when one day he came into the laboratory beaming and said that he'd fallen in love with a French girl he'd met on the street." Massive sniffle. "And you know what?"

"No, what?" Lisa said.

"Back then I was much prettier than that . . . that . . . Juliette Margarine. Just so you know!"

"I see," Lisa said. "But he fell in love with her. That's just how it happens sometimes."

Raspa stopped stirring and cocked her head, looking down at Lisa. "Who died and made you Miss Smarty Pants, if I might ask? You're just a little snippet of a girl. What do you know?"

"Not that much, maybe," Lisa said. "But I lost a friend once, and I made a new one."

Raspa pulled out a handkerchief and blew her nose. "You don't say," she said. "A new friend, huh?"

"Yes," Lisa said. "It's never too late to make new friends, you know."

Raspa sniffled contemptuously. "And who does Little Miss Smarty Pants think would want to be friends with an evil old lady with a wooden leg, if I might ask?"

"Well," Lisa said, looking down at the soap, which was starting to form a nice layer of bubbles, "me, for example."

"Sea spray!" Raspa spluttered, clearing her throat.

Lisa didn't respond. They kept stirring in silence, even though there were enough bubbles now for them to go.

Finally Raspa asked, "Do you know what the stupidest thing is?"

"No," Lisa said.

Raspa laughed a short, hard laugh. "Don't say anything to Victor, but I've known how to make baths that could time-travel the whole time."

Lisa stopped stirring. "What are you saying?"

Raspa shrugged her shoulders. "That I don't actually need his drawings. I can make my own time-travelling bath anytime I want."

"But . . . but why did you follow me and Nilly to Paris if it wasn't to get your claws on those drawings?"

"Isn't that what your friend Nilly would call *elementary*?"

Lisa smiled. "You wanted to find Doctor Proctor, not the drawings for his bath."

Raspa sighed heavily. "I was dumb, I was hoping . . . that maybe there might still be a chance that he would . . ."

"Fall in love with you?"

Raspa laughed a bitter laugh. "Pretty stupid, huh?

I mean, can you imagine? *With me?* An old witch of a woman with a wooden leg and bad breath?"

"I don't know," Lisa said. "But what I don't get is why you're helping Doctor Proctor find Juliette if you don't actually need his drawings after all."

"Sometimes," Raspa said, climbing into the bath, "even witches aren't sure why they do the things they do. Come on, Lisa. Time for us to head to the Dark Ages."

Witching Night

AND, INDEED, THE Dark Ages did turn out to be
extremely dark: coal-black and jet-black, pitch-black
and ink-black. Totally night-time-black, actually. Nilly
determined this as he stood in his bath. Now he cried
out, "Is anyone here?" His voice echoed.

"I'm here," a voice next to him said.

"Well, duh, I know that," Nilly said. "We came in the same bath, didn't we? I was wondering if anyone else was here. Can you see anything?"

"No," Doctor Proctor said. "Juliette? Juliette?"

No answer.

"Juliette!" the professor repeated. "Juli . . . Ow!"

"What was that?"

"Something hit me on the head again."

"What was it?"

"I don't know, but it felt like a bath."

"Is there anyone here?" That was Lisa's voice.

"I'm here," said a hoarse, desert-dry voice.

"Well, duh, I know that," Lisa whispered. "We came in the same bath, didn't we? I was wondering if—"

"We're all here," Nilly said. "But where are we? It's totally impossible to see anything."

"We're exactly where we wanted to be," Doctor Proctor said. "In Joan of Arc's prison cell."

Nilly's eyes started adjusting to the dark, and he

could just make out a little window with bars on it very high up in the wall. And the outlines of three white baths scattered about at random.

"Juliette's been here," Nilly said. "I can see her bath."

There was a creaking squeak.

"The door's closed." That was Raspa's voice. Nilly could just make out her outline over by something that looked like an alarmingly solid iron door.

"Um, so we're locked in and Juliette's not here?" Lisa said. "What are we going to do? Shh! Did you guys hear that?"

Nilly held his breath and listened. All he could hear was a soft crackling from outside, like the sound of fireworks in the distance. But wait! Now he heard it too. A soft moaning. It was coming from . . . from underneath Juliette's bath.

"Help me tip over this bath!" Nilly shouted.

Raspa and Doctor Proctor were at his side in a flash.

They tipped the bath up onto its side and the bathwater poured out onto the black, hard-packed dirt floor. And there, lying on her stomach under the bath, was a woman! The moon must have emerged from the clouds right then, because a pale, flickering glow lit up the prison cell and the woman's auburn hair and white dress.

"Juliette, you . . . !" Lisa started, beaming with joy. But she stopped suddenly when the woman on the floor raised her head and looked at them with her frightened but incandescent blue eyes. Because although she certainly looked like Juliette, with the same colour dress and the same auburn hair, this definitely wasn't Juliette. This was a young woman. Well, actually, she looked like she might just be a teenager.

"Who are you?" Doctor Proctor asked.

"I'm Joan," the girl said, her voice quavering.

"Joan of Arc?" Lisa cried, astonished. The girl had long, beautiful hair, just like in the picture in her history book, but she looked so much younger.

The girl nodded.

Nilly stood frozen in place, still holding the top edge of the bath. He was tongue-tied. The girl under the bath was the most beautiful girl he'd ever seen, more beautiful than the women who had kissed him on the cheek after the bike race, more beautiful than Juliette in that picture from when she and Doctor Proctor were young, and yes, even more beautiful than the cancan dancers at the Moulin Rouge.

"Where's Juliette?" Doctor Proctor asked.

The girl blinked her eyes, not understanding his question.

"The woman who arrived in the first bath!" the professor said.

"I don't know," Joan said, curling up defensively as if she was afraid they were going to hit her.

Finally Nilly let go of the bath, which toppled out of the way with a long, drawn-out boom, and squatted down next to the girl.

"Joan, we know you've been through a lot," he said solemnly in a sort of artificially deep voice as he put his hand on her shoulder. "But you mustn't be afraid of us. We're only here to rescue Juliette. She's the professor's girlfriend. Do you understand?"

The girl nodded at Nilly, who gave her a big smile in return and then added, "As for myself, I'm not seeing anyone at the moment. How about you?"

Lisa cleared her throat and pushed Nilly aside, saying, "Can you tell us what happened, Joan?"

The girl looked from Lisa to Nilly.

"I was sleeping and waiting for them to come and get me," she said. "They're going to burn me at the stake for being a witch today, you know."

"I know," Nilly said, enthusiastically. "Because you helped defeat the English at Orléans."

"Yes," Joan said. "And because I hear God speaking to me. And because I refuse to allow them to give me a bowl haircut."

"A bowl haircut?"

"Yeah, everyone's supposed to wear a bowl haircut. To show that we submit ourselves to God, right? You guys don't have bowl haircuts. That's why they put you in here."

"No," Lisa said. "What Nilly says is true. We time-travelled here from the future in a bath to save Juliette."

Joan stared at them for a long time. "You poor people. They want to burn me at the stake because I claim I've heard a few sentences from God. Guess what they'll do to you when you tell them that ridiculous lie."

"Let's not worry about that now, Joan," Doctor Proctor said. "Just tell us what happened."

"I woke up because someone opened the iron door. That's when I discovered that someone had put a bath on top of me. A second later I heard someone standing up in the bath. The guards were shouting and pulling a wet woman out of the bath and they took her with them. The door slammed shut again and I was alone. I . . . I . . . " her eyes darted from Nilly and Lisa over to the professor, ". . . think maybe they thought she was me in the darkness."

"Oh no," Lisa said. "Do you mean that—"

". . . they came to get my beloved Juliette . . ." a horrified Doctor Proctor continued.

". . . to broil her over a bonfire, like a roast pig?" Nilly gasped.

The girl nodded. "On the square just outside. I'm so sorry . . ."

Something dawned on all of them just then. The flickering light coming in the window way up there on the wall wasn't coming from the moon. And the crackling sound wasn't fireworks. It was a bonfire.

"No!" screamed Doctor Proctor, sinking to his knees. "No!"

Long fingernails dug into Nilly's upper arms and he was raised up. He felt Raspa's deathlike breath on his face. "Up into the crow's nest with you, Napoléon."

A second later he was standing on Raspa's shoulders right in front of the window with the metal bars over it.

"Oh," Nilly said. "Uh-oh."

"What do you see?" Lisa cried impatiently. "Describe what you're seeing."

"Okay," Nilly said. "We're right by the market square here in Rouen. The audience is ready and the players are on the field. And, sure enough, everyone has these unbelievably stupid-looking bowl haircuts. The home team is dressed like priests and they're holding crosses and crucifixes and reciting battle cries from a thick book, probably the Bible. The away team, which consists of only one person, Juliette Margarine, is tied to a stake surrounded by neatly arranged bundles of wood that are just being set on fire. A bunch of torches have been lit around her. Unfortunately the home team looks like the clear favourite. We've got no time to lose . . ."

"Oh no!" Joan cried. "I was the one who was

supposed to be burned. I'm the one who's a witch, not that poor woman!"

Nilly jumped down off Raspa's shoulders, straightened his uniform, put his hand on the hilt of his sabre and proclaimed in a loud voice, "No one is going to be burned here, my dear Joan. Sergeant Nilly is here, and he will get us all out of here and rescue Juliette. First let's check all the bricks in the wall here . . ."

"Why?" the others asked in a chorus of exactly four voices.

"Elementary," said Nilly, who had started feeling his way along the walls with his fingers. "There's always a key or a dagger hidden behind a loose brick in the walls of prisons like this. Haven't you guys ever seen any prison movies? We just have to find the brick."

"Nonsense," Lisa said, but even she couldn't help running her eye along the wall looking for a loose brick.

"Here!" Nilly cried. "Someone wrote something in the mortar over here! This must be the one."

The others came closer. And in the faint moonlight from the little slit high in the wall they saw that, sure enough, there was a date written above the stone.

"A prisoner must have scratched that in," Nilly said, pushing on the bricks around the inscription, but none of them would budge.

"I don't think it was a prisoner," Doctor Proctor said. "Look, here's what it looks like if you scratch something into the mortar." He pulled out a knife and scratched a face with two eyes, a mouth and a Fu Manchu moustache.

"See, the edges are sharp and the surface is rough. But on that date, the letters are smooth, rounded indentations in the cement. That must have been written when the cement was still soft, so, I guess by one of the people who helped build the prison back in 1111."

"Strange," Lisa said.

The others turned to look at her.

"The only person I've ever met who draws little eyes and noses on all his numbers and letters is Nilly."

The others turned to look at him.

"What's your point?" Nilly asked. "I mean, duh, I wasn't around in 1111."

"Eureka!" Doctor Proctor cried.

The others turned to look at him.

"*You* wrote that message," the doctor said. "You were there in 1111! Well, here. You just haven't been there yet!"

And it's funny how two, three and (every once in a while) four brains can suddenly think the same thing at the same time.

"Eureka!" they cried, because "eureka" means that you understand everything.

Raspa poured soap powder into the bath and stirred it while Nilly jumped up onto the edge and got ready.

He was rolling his head around while Doctor Proctor massaged his shoulders and Lisa leaned over to his ear and urged him in a voice that made her sound like she was chanting, "Concentrate on the Old Market Square in Rouen. January thirteenth, 1111. That's when they built this prison. When you get there, get hold of the key to this iron door, get a blacksmith to make a copy, go to the bricklayers in the prison and get them to put it under a brick. Then you write the date in the mortar before it hardens. Okay?"

"Okay, okay," Nilly said.

"Hurry," Joan whispered. She was looking towards the slit where the flickering light was getting brighter and the crackling sound was getting louder.

"The soap is ready," Doctor Proctor said. "Bon voyage! And remember to come back here . . ." He looked at the clock. "Ten seconds from now. At ten fifty-five at night. Hurry!"

"Wait," Raspa said. She stepped forwards and handed

Nilly a small, black leather purse. "This should make it easier to convince the blacksmith and the bricklayers to help you."

"Thanks," Nilly said, stuffing the purse into the pocket of his uniform. Then he shouted, "Cannonball!" and jumped.

The soapy water splashed all the way up to the little window with the bars over it.

"What was in the purse, Raspa?" Doctor Proctor asked quietly as he watched the second hand on the clock.

"Just a formula I happened to discover in my free time," Raspa said. "How to make aurum out of sulphur dioxide, silicon and scrambled eggs."

"Aurum?" Lisa asked.

"Latin for gold," Doctor Proctor said. "Four . . . three . . . two . . . and . . . ZERO!"

They all stared at the bubbles in the bath. No one said anything. Nothing happened. Outside the cheering was starting to get louder.

"Something must have gone wrong in 1111," Raspa said.

Doctor Proctor whispered, barely audibly, "It's too late to go and get him."

"Don't give up!" Lisa said. "He'll be back soon."

Raspa snorted. "What makes you think that?"

"Because he's my friend and I know him," Lisa said. "He's a little forgetful, and he's always a little late. But he'll be here. That's just the way he is."

"Oh no," Joan moaned. They turned round. They followed her eyes towards the little window slit and they could see it too: a tall, clear flame silhouetted against the night sky outside.

Just then they heard the sound of water smacking against water and a voice proclaiming:

"Never go to 1111!"

"Nilly!" Lisa shouted.

"The food is disgusting, the mattresses are filled with straw and fleas, everyone's teeth are rotten and no one has TV!" The red-haired boy was standing on the edge of the bath, looking at them with a triumphant expression.

"Hurry!" Doctor Proctor said. "What took you so long?"

"Sorry," Nilly said, hopping down onto the floor. "But the plague had killed all the blacksmiths in town, so I had to ride a horse to the next village. Then the horse died of the plague on the way back, and I had to walk the rest of the way. And by the time I got back, all the bricklayers had kicked the bucket, so I had to lay the bricks myself. It should be right over . . ."

He pulled his sabre out of the scabbard and was now driving it into the mortar between two of the bricks.

". . . here!"

He bent the blade back, causing small, dry chunks of mortar to fly out. Then he stuck his fingers under the brick, pulled it loose and plucked out the key. He ran over to the iron door, stuck the key in the lock and twisted it. Or rather, he tried to twist it. But the key wouldn't budge.

"Owl poop!" Nilly cursed.

The professor was standing behind him jumping up and down. "What's wrong?!"

"Hm," said Raspa, who was studying the lock. "I'm afraid they've changed the locks since 1111. That was a lot of bricklaying effort for nothing."

"Oh no," said Joan. *For the third or fourth time,* Lisa thought, a little irritated.

"It's hopeless," the professor said, sinking down onto his knees. "Alas!"

"Yup, alas," Nilly said.

But while everyone else was alassing, Lisa had an idea. She walked over to the door, pressed down on the handle and pushed it.

The alassing stopped the instant the unoiled hinges of the door screeched and the door swung open.

"How the . . . ?" started Doctor Proctor.

"Elementary," Lisa said. "If they thought they'd removed the only prisoner who was in here, why would they bother locking the door? Come on!"

"Wait!" Joan yelled. They turned to look at her and saw, to their surprise, that she'd taken out a comb and was now frantically combing her hair. She stopped when she saw the looks of disbelief on their faces.

"Well, there are a lot of people out there, aren't there?" she said, a little miffed, slipping the comb back into her dress.

Then they all rushed out of the door, ran down the dark corridor, up stairs that twisted like snakes round the towers, and finally reached a door that led into a courtyard, which in turn led to the town square.

There they stopped. The reflection of the flames danced on their faces.

"Oh no," Joan said, covering her eyes with her hands.

"We're too late," Doctor Proctor said.

Back to the Present

LISA STOOD AS if frozen. She'd seen this before, in a painting, in a book, a history book.

The flames were licking up around a central stake to which a figure in a white dress was tied.

A man in a priest's robe was standing in front of the bonfire, holding up a cross at her. The people in the square were quiet, all you could hear was the roar of the flames and another priest shouting Latin words up into the night sky. And now Lisa understood everything: why she'd thought Joan of Arc had looked like Juliette Margarine in that painting in her history book. Lisa shuddered. Because she also realised that this could mean only one thing: that what was happening had already happened, that in a mix-up Juliette was going to be burned at the stake today, May 30, 1431, instead of Joan of Arc. That no matter what they did now, it didn't matter. She'd already seen the picture of Juliette in her history book. It was carved in stone. It couldn't be changed.

"It's too late . . ." Lisa whispered. "It's been too late this whole time."

She whispered it so softly that the professor, Nilly and Joan didn't hear it. But Raspa must have heard it, because she leaned over to Lisa and her desert voice blew right by Lisa's ear:

"Maybe so, Lisa. Maybe so. But there's still one thing that can save her."

"Death," Lisa whispered. "You said that a person who was willing to die could change history."

"Correct."

"Doctor Proctor," Lisa said slowly. "He said that he would rather die than lose her."

"He did," Raspa replied. "But it would have to happen before Juliette dies herself."

Lisa bit her lower lip. Juliette's dress had caught fire. Doctor Proctor sank to his knees, sobbing.

"Elementary!" Lisa suddenly exclaimed. "Nilly, do you still have the fartonaut powder?"

But Nilly didn't hear her. He was staring at the bonfire, mesmerised. Lisa stuck her hands down into both pockets of his uniform and pulled out a little plastic sack.

"Is that more time soap bath bomb?" Raspa asked.

"No," Lisa said. "This is an even bigger invention.

One of Doctor Proctor's." Then she tipped her head back, opened her mouth wide, and poured in a good mouthful of the light-blue fartonaut powder.

"What are you doing?" Raspa asked.

"Changing history," Lisa said. "Eight! Tell Doctor Proctor that he should get ready to go and take Juliette's place. Seven!"

"What?"

"Six! Five!"

Nilly, Joan and the professor turned towards Lisa and Raspa.

"Nilly and Joan," Lisa yelled, bending over and aiming her bottom at the bonfire. "Hold on to me tight! Four! Three!"

Nilly understood what his best friend meant right away. As Raspa whispered something in Doctor Proctor's ear, Nilly darted over, grabbed Lisa by one arm and waved to Joan to grab the other.

"Two! One! Zer—"

The noise was so loud that Nilly's ears curled up in gleeful pain, Doctor Proctor felt his skull crunch and Raspa's eyelashes flew off. The flagpoles in the square bent, people toppled over and the priests did somersaults with their robes and adornments flapping around their necks. When they finally recovered their senses, they coughed and blinked their burning, watering eyes, but couldn't see anything. Because the bonfire and all the torches had been blown out and the smoke lay thick over the marketplace in the night-time darkness.

"Nilly!" Lisa yelled in the darkness, coughing.

"Joan!" Nilly yelled in the darkness, coughing.

"Doctor Proctor!" Joan yelled in the darkness, coughing.

But there was no response from Doctor Proctor. Instead they heard voices from the square shouting:

"Light the bonfire again!"

Nilly's hand found another hand.

"Is that you, Lisa?" he yelled. "Talk to me, Lisa!"

A voice very close to his ear whispered, "So girls can't fart, huh? You owe me a ton of sticky caramels."

"Lisa!"

"Come on, let's find Joan."

They fumbled around in the smoke and darkness until Nilly's hands touched a head that suddenly pulled away from him.

"You're messing up my hair!" a voice complained.

"Joan!" Lisa said. "Let's hold hands so we don't lose each other."

But that turned out not to be necessary because the smoke had already started to clear up and they could see the first torches in the square being lit again. And hear voices yelling: "There were some strange people over there and one of them fired off a cannon from their backside. I saw it!"

"Witches and wizards! Get them."

"Get them into the bonfire with that other witch!"

"I think it's about time for us to be going," Nilly said.

"But . . . what about Juliette?" Joan asked.

"And Raspa," Lisa said. "Raspa?"

"Look!" Nilly said, pointing. "Someone's coming."

And sure enough two silhouettes shrouded in smoke came scurrying towards them. One was supporting the other, and they didn't look like priests, bishops or prison guards.

"Run, kids, run!" It was Juliette's voice. "They're right behind us. Back to the cell!"

And so they ran. And as they ran, they heard an unpleasant and now very familiar sound behind them. The crackling sound of firewood burning, the roar of flames devouring wood, the whistle of wind whirling towards the witch's pyre.

"Don't look back, kids!" Juliette shouted.

They did as she said. They didn't look back, just ran. Ran and tried not to think about what was happening to Doctor Proctor on the fire behind them. Ran into the courtyard, through the open door, which they then closed and locked behind them, down the spiral staircase, back down the corridors they'd come through before and, finally, back into the dark prison cell. Lisa held the door open until the last two were in and then she pushed it shut again.

The light from the fire was flickering through the window slit high up on the wall above them.

"Terrible . . ." Joan whispered.

"I have to look!" Nilly said, clutching on to the tall, skinny, soot-blackened form who had entered the room with Juliette. The form positioned itself against the wall and Nilly clambered up onto its shoulders. It wasn't hard to spot. The flames lit up her face . . . Wait! Her? That . . . but that was . . .

Nilly stared in confusion first at the woman on the bonfire, then down at the person whose shoulders he was standing on.

"Doctor Proctor?" Nilly gasped.

"Yes, indeed." The professor sighed.

"But . . . but . . ."

"Raspa had just finished helping me untie Juliette in all the smoke and confusion," the professor said. "I was about to tie myself to the stake when everything went black. After that I'm really not sure what happened."

"But I am," Juliette said. "Raspa knocked Victor out with her wooden leg. I have no idea why. I leaned down over Victor and just barely managed to get him to come to and when I looked up again, Raspa had disappeared in all the smoke. I got Victor back onto his feet and realised I was going to have to drag him back to the prison cell where my bath was so that we could get out of here. And then I spotted you, my dear children . . . You have no idea how relieved I was!"

"Us too," Lisa said. "What do you see out there, Nilly?"

Nilly was staring out through the bars. The flames were now engulfing Raspa's trench coat and wooden leg and her face was glowing red and gold. Nilly wasn't

sure, but it actually looked like she was smiling as she stood there, flashing those sharp teeth of hers. And she was shouting something. It was hard to hear over the roar of the flames, but it sounded like . . . like: "Give me an *L*!"

Nilly shouted as loud as he could through the bars, *"L!"*

Like an echo from far away came, "Give me an *I*!"

"I!"

But then the fire drowned out the rest, and Raspa was engulfed in flames that stretched up and spluttered sparks like shooting stars into the velvety black, strangely beautiful night sky.

Nilly waited a little longer. Then he slid down from the professor's shoulders.

"We don't need to wait for Raspa," he said, sounding unusually subdued for Nilly.

"What?" Joan and Juliette asked.

But Doctor Proctor and Lisa didn't say anything.

The professor looked at Nilly for a long time. Then he nodded slowly at the bath. "Come on, everyone. We have to get out of here before the bubbles are gone."

"Look," Lisa said, pointing down at the dirt floor.

It was Raspa's jar of time soap bath bomb.

"Hm," Doctor Proctor said, holding up the jar. "This means we have enough powder to take a little holiday. I think we need one. What do you all say to a couple days on a sunny Caribbean island, long before it was discovered by the tourist industry?"

WHEN THE TWO prison guards pulled open the door to the cell, all they saw was an empty room with three baths in it.

"What is the meaning of this?" the taller of the two said. Under his helmet he was sporting an unbelievably stupid-looking bowl haircut and on his upper lip he wore a large handlebar moustache.

"Yes, what is the meaning of this?" the other one

said. Under his helmet he had an inconceivably stupid-looking bowl haircut and on his upper lip there wasn't so much as a wisp of hair and no moustache at all.

"Hm," Handlebar said. "There was only one bath in here earlier when we came to get Joan of Arc, not three."

"You're right," No-Moustache said.

"Well," Handlebar said. "It looks like we're never going to find whoever fired that cannon. Come on."

"Hm," said No-Moustache, who was staring at the wall where something had obviously caught his attention.

"What is it?" Handlebar asked, coming over to see.

"This drawing here," No-Moustache said. "That is a really great-looking moustache. I've never seen a moustache like that before, sort of hanging down on the sides like that. I think maybe I'll try to grow—"

"Come on," Handlebar said, pulling No-Moustache out of the cell.

20

India

AZURE BLUE WAVES broke on the white beach where Lisa lay on her back with her eyes closed. Every once in a while she would glance up, and when she did she saw a palm tree silhouetted against a cloudless sky. The palm tree was growing at an angle, leaning out towards the ocean as if it wished it were out there swimming along with Juliette, Doctor Proctor and Joan, who were splashing around in the waves and laughing happily as if nothing had happened. Lisa wished she could join them. But when she thought about Raspa, she just couldn't.

Something blocked out the sun and she opened her eyes. A concerned face with enormous freckles was peering down at her.

"You look concerned," Lisa said.

"Because you seem so preoccupied," Nilly said. "This is supposed to be a holiday. No thinking allowed!"

He was balancing on the sloping trunk of the palm tree, lying on his stomach right over her.

"Do you know why Raspa tied herself to the stake?" Lisa asked.

"Because only death can change history," Nilly said, squinting one eye shut and bending one arm behind his back in a vain attempt to scratch himself between his shoulder blades.

"Yeah, but do you know why she didn't let Doctor Proctor sacrifice his life? Why she took his place?"

"Elementary," Nilly said, trying to scratch himself with his other arm in case maybe it was a little longer. "She loved him."

"You knew?" Lisa asked, amazed.

"Of course. You can always spot love a long way off," Nilly said, wiggling around, sort of like he was trying to roll over onto his back without falling off the tree trunk. "In the end even Raspa managed to see that Doctor Proctor was head-over-heels in love with Juliette. And when she saw Juliette on the bonfire, Raspa knew that the only way she could make the man she loved happy, was to let him have the woman he loved. So she made sure that those two could be together. She sacrificed herself for love, you could say. Just not her own love."

Lisa was touched. "Why, Nilly! And here I was thinking that you boys didn't understand things like this."

"Of course we do," said Nilly, finally successfully lying on his back. He now started pushing himself up and down, scratching his back against the tree trunk.

"Oh, Nilly . . ." Lisa whispered, with a tear in the corner of her eye. "Isn't it wonderful?"

"Yes, it really is," Nilly said, a look of pleasure spreading over his face as he finally succeeded in scratching his itch. "Although things would be nicer here if they served breakfast. A restaurant with a little eggs and bacon would be just the thing. And I didn't think girls could fart!"

"Nilly!" Lisa scolded. "I meant it was wonderful what Raspa did! She didn't have any friends . . . I feel so . . . so . . ." Her eyes filled with tears. "Sorry for her."

"I agree," Nilly said, sticking his finger in his ear and scratching a little in there too, now that he'd started scratching itches. "But you agree that it would be nice to have a little something to eat besides bananas and coconuts that we have to pick ourselves, don't you?"

Lisa didn't respond. She just rolled over onto her stomach and stared at the ocean. They'd been here for three days, and it had been great, but Nilly was right. Out on the horizon a layer of blue-grey clouds had rolled in. Doctor Proctor's skinny, and still just as pale, body came wading back in as he emptied the water out of his motorcycle goggles.

He flopped down on the sand next to them.

"Well, my two best friends," he said. "Everything okay over here?"

They nodded quietly.

"A little homesick, huh?"

They nodded quietly.

"Me too," Doctor Proctor said. "So, did you find any restaurants, Nilly?"

"Nope," Nilly said. "I walked around this whole island, but all I found was a couple of guys who'd just pulled ashore in a rowing boat and asked where they were."

"Oh? Who were they?"

"I don't know. Their English was even worse than mine, but I got that one of their names was Christopher Co . . . Co . . . What's the name of that detective on TV again?"

"Columbo?" Lisa suggested.

"That's it!" Nilly said. "Or something like that. Anyway, I was kidding around with him and I told him this was India. And actually, come to think of it, it seemed like he believed me. At any rate, they jumped back into their rowing boat and rowed super-fast back to a sailing boat that's anchored off shore."

"Hm." Doctor Proctor stood up and glanced over at the three baths that were half-buried in the sand under some palm trees. "I think it's about time to get you two back home to Cannon Avenue before it gets crowded here."

"What do you mean, *you two*?" Nilly said. "Aren't you coming with us?"

"Juliette and I have to go to Paris and settle things with Claude Cliché."

"Without us?" Lisa and Nilly chimed in unison.

"Yes," Doctor Proctor said decisively. "I've exposed you kids to enough danger as it is. I'm a completely irresponsible adult. Didn't you know that?"

"We're quite aware of that," Lisa said. "But you forgot one thing."

"Right," Nilly said.

"We're a team," Lisa said.

"There you have it," Nilly said. "We're a team. And we don't care if everyone else thinks we're a team of pathetic losers. Because we know something they don't know. We know . . . we know . . . uh . . ."

"We know," Lisa took over, "that when friends promise to never stop helping each other, one plus one plus one is much more than three."

Proctor looked at them for a long time. "That was very well put, almost the way I would have said it myself. But—"

"No *buts* about it!" Nilly said. "It *was* you who said it, and you know, that we know, that you know, that there isn't anything you can do, to get us *not* to help you with Claude Cliché."

The professor had to repeat Nilly's sentence silently

to himself a couple of times before he understood what Nilly meant. Then he stared at one of them and then the other, looking defeated. Finally he sighed with resignation. "You really are a couple of stubborn friends."

"Well, what are we waiting for?" Nilly asked. "I'm packed and ready. Lisa?"

Lisa nodded.

"Professor?"

Doctor Proctor nodded.

Nilly sat up on the trunk of the palm tree, balancing carefully and straddling it with his legs. Then he thumped his chest and shouted, "Claude Cliché, here comes the Nillinator!"

21

The Nillinator

NILLY CAUTIOUSLY STOOD up in the bath and looked around. What in the greenest garden? There was no doubt that they were back in the bathroom at the Frainche-Fraille. There was the bath, there was the shelf under the mirror, and there was the toothbrush glass with Perry, the seven-legged Peruvian sucking spider. But that awful sound . . .

"What in the demonic demolition?" whispered Lisa, who had just stood up in the other bath.

"There are enough vibrations in here for twenty jackhammers," said a dripping wet Doctor Proctor.

"It's coming from out there," said Joan, who was already standing over by the door and about to open it as Juliette hissed, "Wait! I know what that is."

The others looked at her.

"That's the sound of hippos snoring."

"Hippos!"

"Yes," Juliette said. "But it's worse than that. Those are the snores of a guy I know much too well."

"Oh no," whispered Doctor Proctor.

"Claude," whispered Lisa, even more softly.

"Cliché," whispered Nilly so softly that no one other than him could hear it over the snoring. He darted over to the door, stretched up onto his tiptoes and peered through the keyhole.

"What do you see?" Proctor asked.

"One . . . two . . . three guys," Nilly said. "They're all sleeping sitting up in chairs. The one next to the radiator has a thin moustache, fat braces with industrial strength clips and looks slipperier than an eel in a bucket of slime."

"That would be Claude Cliché," Doctor Proctor whispered. "What about the other two?"

"They look like . . . well, this might sound a little crazy, but I'm going to go out on a limb and say . . . wait for it . . ." Nilly turned to the others. "Hippopotamuses!"

But strangely enough, it didn't seem like anyone else was surprised by this information. Disappointed at how blasé his audience was, Nilly turned back to the keyhole.

"One is sitting by the window and one has his chair tilted back, propped up against the door to the hallway. In other words, it would be impossible to sneak out without him noticing. And while we're on the topic of bad news, the two hippos each have shotguns in their laps."

Juliette groaned. "They're just waiting for us to come back. And then . . . then . . ."

"That does it!" Doctor Proctor said. He wasn't whispering anymore; instead his voice was trembling with rage. "Step aside, Nilly. The time has come for me to have it out with that man . . ."

"No, Victor!" Juliette said, standing in front of him. "He's not just going to get you. Think of the children. And Joan. The hippos will fill their pockets with coins and chuck them in the Seine."

Proctor stopped. Then he slid down against the side of the bath, holding his head in his hands and moaning in despair. "You're right. What are we going to do?"

"Hm," Juliette said.

"Hm," Lisa said.

"Hm," Joan said.

There was a little *plop* and then Nilly's voice said, "Relax, people! I have a plan."

They stared at Nilly, who studied his index finger with fascination before rubbing it with satisfaction against his trouser leg. "A plan that is as simple as it is ingenious." Nilly unbuttoned his uniform jacket and stuck his hand inside. First he pulled out Marcel's trumpet and set it down, then he stuck his hand in again. "It's already starting to get light outside the window, and it's about time those sleepyheads got a wake-up call they won't soon forget. This plan has already been tested on a certain Mr Napoléon and simply involves pouring a certain powder into the open mouths of the . . . of the . . ." Nilly's facial expression changed as his hand searched around frantically inside his uniform.

"What is it?" Proctor asked. "Did you lose something?"

"There's been a tiny little change in plans, people," Nilly said, smiling stiffly with all of his teeth. "Looks like I left behind the bag of fartonaut powder in Rouen in 1111. But don't worry, Nilly has everything under control. We will simply switch to plan B."

"Which is . . . ?" Lisa asked sceptically.

"For you to trust me."

The other three looked at Nilly, but he didn't say anything else, just spun round on his heels, smiling that weird, crooked smile.

Finally Lisa asked, "Is that the whole plan?"

"Yes," Nilly said, grabbing the tube of Doctor Proctor's Fast-Acting Superglue from the shelf. "Well, that and also I was thinking about playing a little morning reveille. After that I'm going to impofrise."

Lisa slowly shook her head.

"What does 'impofrise' mean, Nilly?" Joan asked.

Nilly flashed her his biggest smile. "That, my dear Joan, means that I, Sergeant Nilly, will come up with new things as soon as the things I already came up with fail."

"We just call that the Nilly Method," Lisa mumbled as Nilly basked in Joan's look of admiration.

"Run out of the door when you hear the trumpet signal," Nilly said, grabbing the trumpet and pushing on the door handle.

"Wait——" Proctor began, but Nilly was already gone.

"What is he doing?" the professor moaned to Lisa, who was holding the door ajar and watching Nilly.

"He's standing in front of one of the hippos, he's squeezing the tube of glue . . . He's smearing glue on the shotgun and the guy's lap. Now he's doing the same thing to the other hippo . . ."

"Go Nilly!" Joan whispered.

"He . . . he's walking behind Claude Cliché's back," Lisa continued. "And . . . and undoing his braces from the back of his trousers . . . and . . . and Claude stopped snoring . . ."

"Oh no!"

"Oh yes. And now . . . Claude is turning over . . . and now . . ."

"Now? What now?"

"Now he's snoring again."

A collective sigh of relief was heard in the bathroom.

"Nilly is tying the ends of his braces to the radiator," Lisa whispered. "There. And now he's climbing up onto the windowsill . . . He's taking a deep breath. He's . . . he's . . ."

The trumpet reveille sliced like a knife through the thunderous snoring, which stopped immediately. Nilly lowered his trumpet and saw three pairs of bulging eyes staring at him.

"Ten hut!" Nilly screamed. "All eyes on me, all feet on deck! Pronto!"

As if on command – which ironically it was – the three men in the room all stood up.

"Get him!" yelled the guy in the braces with the super-skinny moustache.

"Aye, aye, Mr Cliché!" growled one of the hippos as he tried to pull his shotgun off his trouser legs.

"Uh, my gun's stuck!"

"Well then just grab him! He's just a tiny little kid!"

As the hippos lumbered towards him, Nilly saw the bathroom door slide open and his four friends slip out.

"Come and get me, oh you ponderous giants of Dark Continent rivers!" Nilly sang, leaping from the window-sill to the desk chair as the hippos snatched after him. One of them flung himself at the chair, but Nilly hopped up onto the desk.

Furniture was toppled and the lamp smashed during the hippos' waddling quest to nab the red-haired impertinent micro-pipsqueak. Nilly had just made sure that his friends had made it safely out of the door to the hallway, when both hippos came tromping towards him, causing the floor to rock and the light fixture to start swinging. Nilly got a running start, jumped and stretched his arms up towards the ceiling light. If he could just grab it, then he could just swing himself over to the open door and, voilà, he would be safe! He was in midair, laughing to himself. This wouldn't be that hard, he'd seen it done on TV and in movies a zillion times, where the hero just swung through the air like a trapeze artist. The problem was that Nilly's arms . . . well, they were a smidge shorter than most heroes' arms. And the ceiling light was unfortunately hung a little higher than the chandeliers they usually used for this sort of thing in movies.

Nilly's arms spun around, but all his hands came in contact with was air. Everything that goes up must unfortunately come down, and the floor was approaching at high speed.

"Cannonball . . ." Nilly managed to mumble before that little snub-nose of his hit the wood flooring with a crunching sound.

"We've got him," he heard Cliché's voice hiss from the chair by the radiator.

Nilly rolled over and looked up. The two hippos were standing over him.

He heard the jangling of coins.

"Fill his pockets," Cliché's voice hissed. "And toss him out of the window."

Nilly saw the hippo feet approaching. He closed his eyes and felt a hand brush down his side. And then a jerk as the hand found his sabre and yanked it out of its scabbard.

"Get your paws off Nilly, you cud-chewers!"

Nilly opened his eyes. Joan was standing over him with the sabre ready to chop, eyes trained on the hippos.

"You came back," Nilly said.

"I couldn't leave you in the lurch, Nilly," she said calmly. "I mean, I am Joan of Arc, the greatest female warrior in history."

"Joan of Arc? Ha!" They heard Cliché scoff loudly from his seat behind the hippos. "Any idiot knows that she was burned at the stake in 1431. You don't even look like her! Joan of Arc wore lipstick and had a wooden leg and a perm."

"A perm?" Joan screamed, outraged.

"All you have to do is look at the old paintings from when they burned her," Cliché said. "Grab that liar, men!"

The hippos came at her.

More than anything, Nilly wanted to close his eyes, but he kept them open. And he wouldn't regret it. Because what happened next was some of the most amazing stuff he'd ever seen.

Joan swung the sabre with both hands. The weapon swirled so quickly in her hands that he couldn't see the blade anymore, just a watery blur of shimmering steel swishing around. It made small cutting sounds as it sliced through belt buckles, jacket buttons, shirt-sleeves and clumps of hair. Sideburns, fringes and side partings vanished.

When Joan was done, the two hippos were standing

in front of her, stunned, with their trousers round their ankles, bare arms sticking out of sliced-off jacket and shirt sleeves and the ugliest bowl haircuts Nilly had seen since the Dark Ages.

"There's your perm!" Joan screamed. "Come on, Nilly!"

She pulled Nilly to his feet and dragged him behind her out of the door.

As they ran down the stairs, they could hear Cliché yelling. "Give me the shotgun! Well then, take off your trousers and give me those too, you idiot!"

Joan and Nilly ran down all the flights of stairs, past the pictures of the Trottoir family, past the armchairs in the lobby, past the reception desk where Monsieur Trottoir just managed to ask, "Checking out?" before they were out of the revolving door and onto the cobblestones in front of the building.

"Over here!"

They spotted Doctor Proctor, Lisa and Juliette, who

were waiting for them on the other side of the market square next to a couple of empty fruit stalls.

"Watch out!" Lisa yelled.

Just then they heard a breathless voice right behind them say, "Freeze, otherwise I'll shoot you to smithereens!"

Joan and Nilly stopped. And turned round.

Cliché was standing just a few metres behind them with his shotgun aimed directly at them. A pair of hippo trousers was still hanging from the shotgun.

Cliché was leaning over slightly, as if there was a strong headwind, and it was easy to see why. His braces – which ran from the waistband of his trousers over his stomach and shoulders and back in through the revolving doors into the Hôtel Frainche-Fraille behind him – were stretched as tight as guitar strings. Those really were some good, solid braces clips that Cliché had earned his fortune from!

"Come a little closer, so I can be sure I'll hit you, you

little gnome!" Cliché screamed at Nilly as he curled his finger round the shotgun trigger.

"I'd love to help you out there, Monsieur Cliché," Nilly said. "But considering you're the one doing the shooting and I'm the one who's going to be doing the dying, I think it makes the most sense for *you* to take a few steps closer to *me*."

"You badly mannered rascal!" Cliché growled, forcing his way another step closer as his braces trembled and whimpered in protest, but Cliché was so worked up that he didn't notice what seemed to be holding him back.

"I am a *very* small target, so maybe just one more step, Mr Barometer." Nilly smiled tauntingly.

"Prepare to be decimated!" Cliché said, raising his foot to take another step.

But that was it. And, oh, what an *it* it was. A strange expression came over Monsieur Cliché's face as he felt himself losing his balance as his body was pulled backwards with such force that the speed of the pulling kept increasing. Cliché flew backwards through the revolving door so fast that he was no longer touching the ground. He flew past the reception desk where Monsieur Trottoir only had a chance to inhale before asking, "Checking in?", past the armchairs, up the stairs, past the Trottoir family pictures and in through the open door of the hotel room, where the back of his head struck the radiator so hard that the clang sounded as if someone had just rung the biggest bell in Notre Dame cathedral.

And, as the clang was still reverberating across the city, our friends saw two terrified hippo-like guys dressed in only tattered rags and underwear run out of the Hôtel Frainche-Fraille and disappear round the nearest corner.

"Whoa, what did you guys do to them?" Lisa asked. "Those were the worst bowl haircuts I've ever seen."

"Not *us*," Nilly said, and pointed at Joan. *"Her."*

"I just impofrised a little," Joan said.

"And now . . ." Doctor Proctor said, picking up the shotgun that Cliché had dropped, ". . . shall we pay Barometer Cliché a bedside visit?"

CLICHÉ WAS LEANING slumped against the radiator and looked like he was still unconscious when they entered the room. He wasn't snoring, but breathed steadily while his eyelids fluttered occasionally.

"I'm sure he'll come round soon," Doctor Proctor said. "As we now know, it's almost impossible to change history. Cliché is and will stay married to Juliette, and he'll never willingly grant her a divorce. Any suggestions on what we can do?"

"Run away," Lisa said. "You guys could live in Cannon Avenue."

Proctor shook his head. "Cliché and his hippos will find us no matter where we go."

Juliette buried her face in her hands. "Oh, I wish he would have amnesia when he wakes up, that he would forget about being barometer, forget about me, forget that we were ever married."

"Hm," Nilly said. Then he stood up and went into the bathroom.

"Well, he did hit his head awfully hard," Proctor said. "But I'm afraid a total loss of memory is too much to hope for."

"Leave it to me," Nilly said, coming out of the bathroom with the toothbrush glass in his hand. "And to Perry."

"Perry?" Joan asked, staring at the little spider inside the glass.

"A seven-legged Peruvian sucking spider." Nilly walked over to the unconscious man and set the open end of the glass against his ear. And, voilà, the little spider was gone.

"What are you doing?" Juliette asked, appalled.

"The question you should be asking is, 'What is *it* doing?' Because since Perry is a sucking spider, he's inside this man's head right now, sucking up all his memory. When the man wakes up, he'll feel like he had a good night's sleep. He'll be in fine form and a great mood. However, the only thing he'll be sure of is that he isn't able to remember anything. Not a thing. Nothing. Nada."

Nilly looked around at the sceptical faces.

"It's true!" Nilly said indignantly. "It's all described in detail in *AYWDE*."

"AYWDE?" Juliette asked.

"An abbreviation for *Animals You Wish Didn't*—"

"Nilly!" Lisa groaned. "Those animals in that book are just things that you made up!"

"They most certainly are not!" Nilly said, crossing his arms and looking profoundly insulted. "But if you guys would rather, you could just use the Cliché method. Fill his pockets with coins and chuck him in the river!"

Doctor Proctor shook his head. "That's what makes us different from people like him, Nilly. We don't do things like that."

"All right," Nilly said, disgruntled. "So skip the part about the coins and just toss him in the river. That would be a lot cheaper too."

"Nilly!"

Nilly stomped his foot angrily against the floor. "But you guys know it will be impossible to get him sent to jail. There isn't a judge in Paris who would dare to convict him! And when he comes to, he'll—"

"Eureka!" Lisa shouted.

The two grumpmeisters turned to stare at her. Because they knew that Lisa wasn't the kind of person who shouted "eureka" everyday.

"Jail," Lisa said.

"What do you mean?" Proctor asked.

"We'll do what Raspa did with Juliette! We use the bath to send him to a jail in a time that's far, far away."

"Perfect!" Nilly said. "And when he comes round, he won't remember how he got there and won't be able to explain that he's innocent!"

Proctor, on the other hand, did not look as enthusiastic. "I'm not so sure taking the law into our own hands like that is the right thing to do. I mean, we're not judges."

"Well, do you have a better idea?" Nilly asked.

"No," Proctor admitted.

"We could send him somewhere where he could stay until we have a chance to think of something," Lisa said. "Then we could go back and get him later."

Everyone thought this was a good idea, so they set to work. They undid Cliché's braces, and with them all working together they managed to get him into the bathroom and up into the time-travelling bath.

As they were doing this, there was a cautious knock

on the door to the hotel room, and Juliette went to open it.

"Where should we send him?" Lisa asked.

"Leave it to me," Nilly said, clutching the jar of time soap bath bomb. "I know a really clever place."

Juliette stuck her head into the bathroom. "There's someone here to see you, Victor. And you, Lisa."

"Hm," Proctor said. "Who could it be?"

"A French woman who knows you both," Juliette said. "She says she's an assistant judge."

"I don't know any French women," Lisa said. "And certainly no judges, assistant or otherwise."

"Don't be so sure," Juliette said with a wink.

Lisa and Proctor walked out of the bathroom and, sure enough, there was an elegant adult woman. She was wearing the kind of business attire that makes you look thinner than you are, and the kind of glasses that make you look like you don't really need glasses. There was something vaguely familiar about her.

Behind her there were two uniformed policemen. They each had a different kind of moustache. Enough said.

"*Bonjour*, Lisa." The woman in the suit smiled, held out her hand and said something else in French.

"Uh . . ." Lisa said, jumping a little as Juliette decisively slid her French nose clip back into place.

"You don't recognise me, do you?" the woman said. "Without the poncho."

"Uh, no," Lisa said.

"What if I take these off?" the woman asked, taking off her glasses.

Then Lisa saw it.

Sure enough, she wasn't a little girl anymore, she was a grown woman, but it was . . . Yes, it was the girl she'd met by the bridge outside Innebrède!

"Anna?" Lisa exclaimed.

"Yup, it's me," the woman laughed. "I suppose I ought to be surprised to see you again too, but my whole life I've had this feeling that we would see each other again. Especially since I made a decision that day we met by that bridge."

"Oh?"

"Do you remember what we talked about?"

"Hm . . . Wait, yes! How terrible it was that no one was brave enough to stop men like Claude Cliché."

"Exactly. But you said *I* ought to try. So I decided I would. I worked hard in school, I studied the law in Paris and I've worked long and hard until now to become a judge. For the last year I've been leading the investigation into Claude Cliché. We've had him under surveillance day and night to obtain evidence of his criminal activities. We decided a few days ago that we have enough to arrest him, so we decided to apprehend him when he came here today."

"That's great!" Lisa said, clapping her hands. "Did you hear that, Doctor Proctor? Now we don't need to send Cliché anywhere." Lisa turned back to Anna again. "Because you guys promise to put him away for a good, long time, right?"

"Yup, we promise," said Anna Showli. "He's going to spend a lot of years in jail, especially now that we witnessed firsthand his attempts to shoot that unbelievably cute little boy outside. That boy sure is a quick thinker, I have to say."

"He is *very* quick," the professor chuckled.

"We're free!" Juliette cheered and kissed Proctor on the mouth causing his face to go completely red.

"Yippee!" cheered Joan.

Lisa wanted to cheer too, but one word Proctor had said had set off alarms in her head.

One of the policemen cleared his throat. "Well, why don't we see about arresting this scoundrel?"

"Yup, enough talk," the other one said, walking over to the bathroom door and opening it.

"What is that kid doing?" the first policeman asked. "Is he washing his hair? Now?"

"And where's Claude Cliché?"

Right then Lisa thought of the word. *Quick*. Nilly was *quick*. Uh-oh.

The policemen jumped back a step as the little boy flipped his head back up out of the foaming bathwater, blew the soap away from under his nose, exhaled and announced, "It's done!"

His smile stretched from ear to ear below his dripping, bright red fringe.

"You didn't . . . did you . . . ?" Juliette started.

"I must say, I did," Nilly laughed. "I bet we won't see that guy again for a while."

"Well then, we have to go back and get him," Proctor said. "They're here to arrest him right now."

"Oh?" Nilly asked. "Cool. Uh, but then I think we'd better hurry. I forgot all about the part where we go back to get him and, uh, I'm afraid I used up the rest of the time soap bath bomb."

"Oh dear," Proctor said. "Well, well, then, we'd

better hurry up and go back while there are still enough bubbles in the bath. I'll go myself and . . ."

But Lisa had already seen it. Seen the familiar zigzag smile on Nilly's face, the one that meant that yet another plan had gone down the drain. Which is why Lisa wasn't at all surprised when Nilly opened his hand, showing them the plug, and right then they heard the slurping sound of the last of the soapy water disappearing down the drain.

"I guess I was a little, uh, quick," Nilly said.

There was absolute silence in room four at the Hôtel Frainche-Fraille. Everyone just stared at Nilly. And the silence continued. For a long time. A very long time.

Until Nilly eventually said, "Well, well," and brushed his hands together. "What's done is done. Anyone else feel like some breakfast?"

Tokyo

CLAUDE CLICHÉ WOKE up trying to breathe underwater. And since it is widely acknowledged that breathing underwater doesn't work particularly well unless you're a fish or other marine animal, he was basically drowning and started automatically flailing his arms and legs. And then, just like that, he managed to inhale some air after all and discovered that his head was now above water and that he was sitting in a bath. There were trees around him. Tall tree trunks with vines dangling between them. The trunks disappeared up into a very green, very dense canopy of leaves way above him. He was in a jungle, of that there was little doubt.

But how in the world had he got here, in a bath of all things? Cliché furrowed his brow and struggled to remember. He tried to remember who he was, where he came from and what had been happening before he woke up in this bath with a frightful headache.

And do you think he could remember anything? Him, a man with a spider – that may or may not have been a seven-legged Peruvian sucking spider – in his ear and possibly even further in?

Well, here's the answer:

He remembered everything. Absolutely everything.

He remembered, for example, that his name was

Claude Cliché, that he was a barometer and that he owned a lot of stuff. Among other things, he owned a whole heap of money, the patent for a braces clip, a village full of hippos, a castle called Margarine and a baroness named Juliette. He remembered that he had been sitting in the Hôtel Frainche-Fraille in the room of that stupid inventor Juliette thought she was in love with. And he remembered *quite* clearly the little red-haired boy who was dressed like Napoléon and the girl who claimed she was Joan of Arc. Yup, they had tricked him! Their reward for that would be a lot of small change and a trip to the bottom of the Seine.

Cliché stood up and climbed out of the bath. He wasn't the least bit scared. Not at all! He was the King of Paris, wasn't he? No matter how far into this jungle he might be, it was only a question of time until he was back home again. And then he would start hunting!

He started walking towards a clearing in the trees.

As he approached, he heard some sounds, like buzzing and clicking.

Could it be ticking tigers, hiccupping hyenas or rattlesnakes?

Or the clicking of crocodile jaws clacking together?

Ha! It didn't scare him. Cliché marched straight ahead, bending the branches aside.

And there, right in front of him, were the creatures making the buzzing and clicking sounds.

Buzzz-click! Buzzz-click!

Claude started laughing out loud.

It was a huge group of Japanese tourists standing behind some bars that obviously formed some kind of cage. The Japanese tourists were taking pictures with little cameras. *Buzzz-click!* How comical! When they caught sight of Claude, they were suddenly scared and started talking to each other in a strange, staccato-sounding language.

"Boo!" Claude yelled at them, because he liked it

when people were afraid of him. And now he was in high spirits, because behind the people, above the trees, he could see skyscrapers. And where there were skyscrapers, the nearest airport couldn't be far away.

"This isn't over, Doctor Proctor . . ." he mumbled to himself, rubbing his hands together. But just then he discovered to his astonishment that the cage in front of him continued around to his right and to his left. Which meant that he – and not the Japanese photographers – was in the cage. Hm. Whatever, same difference! Now it was just a matter of finding the door out of this darned cage.

"Hey, where's the door?" Cliché yelled, but the people on the outside of the bars just stared at him. Or rather they actually weren't staring at *him*. They were staring over him, he thought. And they'd stopped taking *buzzz-click!* pictures with their cameras. In the silence that resulted, Cliché heard a familiar sound: snoring. But not the snoring of hippopotamuses. Something

that must be even bigger. And just then a big shadow fell over him.

Cliché just had time to look up, just had time to think, just had time to understand how his story was going to end. When it did.

The ground shook and clouds of dust rose up as the enormous, snoring creature – and Claude Cliché for that matter – hit the ground. The cage shook so the iron sign on the outside came off, fell down, and rolled sideways down an asphalt path in the Tokyo Zoo.

Then it was quiet again. The only thing you could hear was the ringing of the iron sign which had stopped rolling and tipped over with a clanging sound, right in front of the feet of a little girl who had just walked up holding her father's hand. And since the sign landed with the words up and the little girl had just learned how to read, she read it, faltering only a little, out loud to her father:

"Cong . . ."

"Yes," her father said.

"Congolese . . ."

"Good," said her father.

"Congolese Tse-Tse . . ."

"You're doing really well!" her father encouraged.

"Congolese Tse-Tse Elephant!"

"Did you hear that!" the father exclaimed to the other observers, who were still looking on in terror. "My daughter is only four years old and she can read! My child is a genius!"

"Golly," said one of the tourists.

Someone raised a camera.

Buzzz-click!

23

Home Again

"BOAN SWOIR!"

It was Sunday afternoon and Lisa's parents looked up from their books to smile at their daughter, who was suddenly standing in the doorway to the living room chirping hello to them in French.

"Boan swoir yourself," her father the Commandant replied. "Did you have a good time in Sarpsborg?"

"I'm so happy to see you guys again," Lisa said, going over first to her father and then her mother and giving them each a good, long hug.

"Well that was an enthusiastic hug," her mother laughed. "Did Anna's father give you a lift back here? I thought I heard a car engine outside."

"That was Doctor Proctor's motorcycle," Lisa said. "I ran into him on my way back and he gave me a lift. Nilly and I are invited to dinner in his garden. Is that okay?"

"Of course," her mother said. "Just don't stay out too late, it's a school night. Did you practise your clarinet? You've got band practice tomorrow, you know."

"Oops. I'll do that now."

Lisa dropped her backpack on the floor and ran up to her room, and soon her parents heard the reedy hollow sound of a clarinet playing . . . Could that be the Marseillaise?

"Do you know what I like best about living in

Cannon Avenue?" the Commandant asked, humming along to the melody. "That it's so safe and boring here, you don't have to worry about anything at all happening."

JULIETTE, LISA AND Nilly were sitting at the picnic table in the tall grass under the pear tree in Doctor Proctor's garden, waiting. They cheered when they saw Doctor Proctor emerge from the house balancing a tray with a two-metre-long jelly on it.

"Help yourselves," he said, plunking the tray down onto the table.

Nine minutes later they were all leaning back, their stomachs bulging, wearing satisfied grins.

"I just talked to Joan on the phone," Juliette said. "Unfortunately, she didn't get that hairdresser's job at Montmartre. The lead stylist thought her methods were a little, uh, dramatic. And bowl haircuts haven't come back in style yet."

"It's just a matter of time," Nilly said.

The other three didn't respond, just silently and sceptically eyed the bright red bowl haircut Joan had given Nilly as a goodbye present along with a kiss in the middle of his freckled nose.

"What are you looking at?" Nilly said. "Trendsetters have to lead the way, right?"

"Anyway." Doctor Proctor chuckled. "She got another job. Didn't she, Juliette?"

"Yup," Juliette said. "As a tourist guide at the Museum of the History of France at the Palace of Versailles. She's going to tell people about the Middle Ages and especially about the famous Joan of Arc, who led the French in battle against the English and was ultimately burned at the stake. The museum director was very impressed at her detailed knowledge."

The professor cleared his throat: "As long as we're on the subject of friends who are no longer with us. Before you guys came over, I took a spin down to Rosenkrantz Street and the Trench Coat Clock Shop."

Everyone looked at him.

"The clock shop wasn't there," Proctor said. "There was an old jewellery store there instead."

"Old?" Nilly burst out. "Impossible! The Trench Coat Clock Shop was there last Friday!"

The professor nodded. "I know. But according to an old cab driver who was parked nearby, the jewellery store had been there since he was a kid. And he'd never heard of a Trench Coat Clock Shop."

They sat in silence for a while, everyone lost in his own thoughts. When Lisa went to take a bite of her jelly, she was surprised to find that her plate was empty. She looked over at Nilly, who looked at her with innocent blue eyes, but puffed-out balloon cheeks, as he hurriedly tried to swallow the last of the evidence.

"Nilly!" she said. "You ate mine!"

His response was drowned out by all the jelly dribbling out of the corners of his mouth.

"Huh?" Lisa asked.

Nilly tilted his head back and repeated, "Sho shue me!"

The professor, Juliette and Lisa couldn't help but laugh at that.

Then they started retelling all the fantastic things they'd experienced over the last two days. Or the last nine hundred years. Depending on how you looked at it. About Nilly who had ridden in the Tour de France and called off the Battle of Waterloo. About Lisa who had designed the Eiffel Tower and blown out a whole witch's pyre with her fart. About Doctor Proctor who was almost beheaded, but saved at the last minute by some clever trumpet playing. And about Juliette who was finally free and hadn't heard a peep from Cliché.

"Cheers!" Doctor Proctor said sincerely, and they all raised their glasses of pear juice. "Not to changing history, but to changing the future."

And they drank to that. But there was no longer any future for this jelly or this Sunday evening. The tray in front of them was bare, the moon had risen and the birds that had settled on the pear tree to listen to all their incredible exploits were starting to yawn.

So they said good night and Proctor and Juliette went into the blue house, Lisa into the red and Nilly into the yellow.

In her room Lisa thought about the clock shop that was gone and how, well, how it was like it had never existed. She decided to look through her schoolbooks until she found her history book, flipped to the chapter on Joan of Arc, and looked at the famous painting of her death. And gasped in shock even though she was half expecting it.

The picture had changed.

The woman didn't have long auburn hair anymore, but inky black hair. She was wearing red lipstick, had long fingernails with red fingernail polish, and down — under her dress — wasn't that . . . a roller skate?

Lisa gulped and thought about Raspa, who had given her life for love. And maybe also to make up for everything she'd tried to destroy. Lisa remembered something that Nilly had told Mrs Strobe in school back at the beginning of this story:

"To be a real hero, you have to be really dead."

Lisa decided that tomorrow she would copy and enlarge the picture of Raspa and hang it up on the wall over her bed. Not just because it was a truly magnificent picture and everyone knew that the woman in the fire was a hero, but because it would remind Lisa of something important. That even if a person did something wrong, it was never – never – too late to fix it again. When you thought about it that way, anyone could change history at least a little bit at any time.

Then Lisa closed her history book and looked over at Nilly's bedroom window.

And sure enough, the shadow play had begun. It clearly depicted a little boy and a slightly bigger woman dancing the cancan and every once in a while kissing a little. Lisa giggled. You would almost think Nilly was in love. And now he was standing on his bed and he started jumping up and down. The shadow, which was twice as big as the tiny little boy, did a somersault, and Lisa laughed so hard she hiccupped. Laughed so hard she cried. Laughed so hard she had to put her head down on her pillow and close her eyes. And when she did that, she fell asleep.

DOCToR PROCTOR'S F.A.R.T. POWDER